Slade felt the ru

away from him.

"You seem to want to be alone," Kaitlin said, her voice a sweet whisper.

"Not tonight," he replied. "C'mon and sit with me awhile."

She stood there, hesitating. He could almost feel the conflicting thoughts rushing through her head. He felt the same kind of warning each time he was around the woman.

But she moved, finally. She went to the kitchen and put the glass in the sink and stood there for a minute staring out the window. Then she let out a gasp. "Slade?"

"What?"

"I...I think there's someone out there."

TEXAS K-9 UNIT:

These lawmen solve the toughest cases with the help of their brave canine partners

Tracking Justice–Shirlee McCoy, January 2013
Detection Mission–Margaret Daley, February 2013
Guard Duty–Sharon Dunn, March 2013
Explosive Secrets–Valerie Hansen, April 2013
Scent of Danger–Terri Reed, May 2013
Lone Star Protector–Lenora Worth, June 2013

Books by Lenora Worth

Love Inspired Suspense

A Face in the Shadows
Heart of the Night
Code of Honor
Risky Reunion
Assignment: Bodyguard
The Soldier's Mission
Body of Evidence
Lone Star Protector

Love Inspired

†*The Carpenter's Wife*
†*Heart of Stone*
†*A Tender Touch*
Blessed Bouquets
"The Dream Man"
**A Certain Hope*
**A Perfect Love*
**A Leap of Faith*
Christmas Homecoming
Mountain Sanctuary
Lone Star Secret
Gift of Wonder
The Perfect Gift
Hometown Princess
Hometown Sweetheart
The Doctor's Family
Sweetheart Reunion
Sweetheart Bride

Steeple Hill

After the Storm
Echoes of Danger
Once Upon a Christmas
"'Twas the Week Before Christmas"

†Sunset Island
*Texas Hearts

LENORA WORTH

has written more than forty books for three different publishers. Her career with Love Inspired Books spans close to fifteen years. In February 2011 her Love Inspired Suspense novel *Body of Evidence* made the *New York Times* bestseller list. Her very first Love Inspired title, *The Wedding Quilt,* won *Affaire de Coeur*'s Best Inspirational for 1997, and *Logan's Child* won an *RT Book Reviews* Best Love Inspired for 1998. With millions of books in print, Lenora continues to write for the Love Inspired and Love Inspired Suspense lines. Lenora also wrote a weekly opinion column for the local paper and worked freelance for years with a local magazine. She has now turned to full-time fiction writing and enjoying adventures with her retired husband, Don. Married for thirty-six years, they have two grown children. Lenora enjoys writing, reading and shopping…especially shoe shopping.

Lone Star Protector

Lenora Worth

HARLEQUIN® LOVE INSPIRED® SUSPENSE

Special thanks and acknowledgment to Lenora Worth for her contribution to the Texas K-9 Unit miniseries.

Recycling programs for this product may not exist in your area.

ISBN-13: 978-0-373-44540-0

LONE STAR PROTECTOR

This edition published by arrangement with Love Inspired Books.

www.LoveInspiredBooks.com

Printed in U.S.A.

Cursed be he that smiteth his neighbor in secret.
And all the people shall say, Amen.
—*Deuteronomy* 27:24

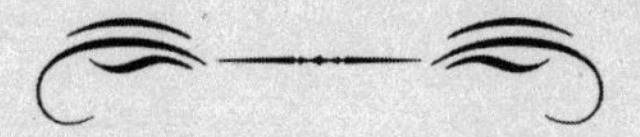

To K-9 officers and their canine partners. Thanks for your hard work and willingness to serve. It was a joy to learn more about what you do every day.

ONE

"Don't make a sound."

K-9 trainer Kaitlin Mathers felt the cold nozzle of the gun sticking into her rib cage, shock and fear pouring through her system like a hot, blowing wind. The man holding her had a raspy voice and wore silky black coveralls and a black ski mask, even though it was June in Southwest Texas. She could feel his sweat breaking through the lightweight material of his clothes, could smell a musky scent that probably came from the heat and high adrenaline. When she tried to squirm away, something cold and metal pressed against her backbone. A zipper, maybe? Determined to keep it together, Kaitlin didn't move or try to speak. She had to stay calm so she wouldn't be killed. So she could get away.

Across the K-9 training yard, Warrior barked and snarled from his vantage point inside his mesh kennel porch. Thankfully, she hadn't put the young trainee inside for the night yet. Someone would hear the barking and come around the corner, wouldn't they? *Please, Lord, give me courage,* she prayed, memories of her mother's death playing through her head.

That's what you get for working late all by yourself. You're more like your mother than you realized. But it had never occurred to Kaitlin that someone would be hiding in the bushes right outside the doors of the Sagebrush K-9 Training Facility. Especially since the building and training yard were located inside a locked fence directly behind the Sagebrush Police Department.

The man holding her must have known the risks, but he'd somehow managed to get through that gate. He hurriedly shoved her toward a waiting van, the same dark van she'd only minutes before noticed parked underneath an old oak near the back parking lot.

"I need you to come with me," he said, his whisper like a knife slicing through her nerve endings.

"Why?" She had a right to ask.

"I'll explain that later, sweetheart."

Kaitlin looked at the van, then tried to look back at her attacker. She caught a glimpse of strange, black eyes, another shock wave jolting through her system. Before she could see anything else, he jerked her back around and pushed the gun hard against her side. "Let's go."

Kaitlin didn't think about being silent anymore. If she got in that van, the chances were very good that she'd be dead by nightfall. *Just like Mom.* But unlike her too-trusting mother, Kaitlin didn't intend to become a victim. She screamed and started fighting for her life.

K-9 captain Slade McNeal was halfway to his vehicle when he heard barking. Excited barking. Whirling toward the kennels, he wondered which dog had been left inside them.

Warrior.

He'd just watched trainer Kaitlin Mathers putting the newbie, a strong Belgian Malinois that reminded him of his own missing German shepherd, Rio, through his paces. They'd spoken briefly, and he'd gone back to his office.

But where was Kaitlin now? It wasn't like her to leave

a dog unattended, even kenneled. Warrior was sure upset about something.

The dog kept on barking, the sounds growing more urgent. Something was up. Slade hurried toward the building, his weapon drawn. He passed the kennels but didn't see anyone. Since Warrior would have a close bond with Kaitlin, it made sense that the dog was trying to warn her about something. Or alert someone else.

"Good job," Slade said when he passed the pacing, snarling animal. He didn't try to stop Warrior's barking.

Then he heard a scream, followed by grunts and shouts.

Slade stood at the corner of the building, then pivoted around the side, his weapon still drawn. About twenty yards away, a man in a dark mask had Kaitlin by the arm, trying to drag her across the asphalt toward an open black van. And he had a gun pointed at her head.

Slade's heart rushed ahead, pumping adrenaline right along with realization. He recognized this man. The Ski Mask Man, they'd labeled him around headquarters. Slade had been gunning for this guy for five long months. This criminal had some nerve, trying to kidnap a trainer right out of the training yard.

A multitude of angry memories raced through Slade's head, followed by the taste of victory. Could this case finally get a break? He glanced back at Warrior, then turned his attention back to the scene in front of him. He'd never make it to the locked cage to let the dog out, and he didn't have time to dig for his keys or call for backup. He could shoot the lock, but what if he hit the dog?

He'd have to do this on his own. "Drop the weapon!" Slade shouted. "Now!"

Kaitlin gulped a breath of relief. Slade was here. She kept telling herself that over and over. She also kept telling herself that she could handle this because she'd been trained as a police officer. She might be a little rusty since becoming a full-time trainer, but she'd find a way out of this. Somehow. She wouldn't end up like her mother.

Surprised at Slade's command, the man holding her pivoted toward Slade, his gun still aimed at Kaitlin. She pulled away, but he held her tight against him, his low whisper a warning. "Do you want to live?"

She did want to live, but Kaitlin wasn't going without a fight. She'd rather take her chances right here in the training yard with Slade McNeal than go anywhere with this man. Captain McNeal knew his job, and he was good at that job. He'd get them both out of this, and she'd find a way to help him.

Slade advanced a few steps. "Drop the weapon and let her go."

The man tightened his hold, but Kaitlin could feel the apprehension and indecision in his actions. Did he know the captain? She used the brief distraction to dig in her heels, kicking and hitting and screaming. Taking a chance, she elbowed the man in his side, then wrapped her leg behind his to trip him, causing him to lose the grip on his weapon. The gun slipped out of his grasp and hit the hot pavement. He cursed and grabbed Kaitlin again, holding her like a shield in front of him, his strong grip twisting her shoulders back so hard she cried out in pain.

"I'm taking her with me," the man shouted.

Behind Slade, Warrior was going wild against the confines of his big wire-front cage, his barks frantic and snarling. Kaitlin watched, afraid for Slade. The K-9 captain held his gun on her attacker and kept advancing, inch by inch.

"Let her go," Slade shouted again over the barking dog, his finger on the trigger of his Glock 22 service revolver. "Don't make me shoot you!"

The man stopped tugging and glared at Slade. Holding Kaitlin with one hand, he tried to reach down and scoop up his gun with the other. He seemed to know Slade wouldn't take the shot with her shielding him.

Kaitlin glanced at Slade, then using all of her strength, kicked the weapon out of her abductor's reach and, with a grunt, yanked herself away. She fell, the concrete scraping through her khaki pants to tear at her knee. But she scrambled to her feet and did a quick run toward some shrubbery near the building. That left the culprit in full view and diving for his gun. Slade could take the shot and kill the man right where he stood. Kaitlin went on her knees behind the shrubbery, watching as Slade pulled off a round, hitting near where the gun lay, causing the perp to jump and roll.

"Don't move," Slade shouted as he starting walking. "I will hit the mark next time."

Kaitlin held her breath, praying Slade wouldn't get shot. She should have picked up the gun. But the attacker took his own chances. He grabbed for his weapon, then pivoted and rolled into a ragged hunched-over zigzag toward the van, firing behind himself as he ran.

Helpless, Kaitlin watched from the bushes, her heart caught in her throat. But while she watched, she tried to memorize everything she could about her attacker.

She held a hand to her mouth, watching as Slade dived to the ground to avoid being hit, but got off a couple of rounds before the man returned fire. One of Slade's shots hit the side of the van, but missed the moving target. The suspect did a nosedive into the open vehicle and the van spun around in Reverse and took off. Two of them. He'd had a getaway driver.

Slade took one more shot, but the van swerved and skidded out onto the side street, then the driver gunned it and disappeared into the burnt dusk. Slade squinted into the sunset, trying to see the tag numbers. All he saw was a temporary tag with smeared letters and numbers. He couldn't get a read on it.

Nothing to do there. He got on the radio and alerted the switchboard operator. "McNeal, K-9 Unit 601, 207-A averted, back parking lot behind the training yard. Suspect got away. All clear."

Holstering his weapon, he hurried to where Kaitlin still sat pressing her entire body in between the prickly shrubbery and the building bricks, her eyes bright with fear and relief. This whole event had lasted a couple of minutes, but it sure felt like a lifetime.

"Hey, you okay?" he asked, placing a hand on one of her arms. With a gentle tug, he pulled her out of the shrubbery.

She jerked away, then looked up at him. "Slade?"

"Yeah, it's me. They're gone. You're safe now."

She nodded and then plowed into his arms and held on for dear life. "Thank you." Her voice was shaky but getting stronger with each inhale of breath. "Thank you."

Slade allowed her to hug him close, his fingers hovering in the air before he put his arms around her shoulders and patted her on the back. "You're all right now. It's over."

The woman in his arms clung to him for a while longer.

Slade didn't try to pry her away. Her whole body seemed to tremble against him. His own heart echoed that trembling, but maybe for an entirely different reason. It had been a long time since he'd held a woman so close. But it hadn't been so long that he could get past the image of his wife walking out the door and getting in that car.

He wanted to hold Kaitlin and comfort her, but bitter memories tinged with regret pulled him back.

Besides, he knew if anyone saw this, they'd both have some explaining to do. And with a K-9 dog barking and shots fired in the back of police headquarters, the entire department would be rushing around the building any moment now.

He backed up, took her by her arms and set her a few inches away. "Kaitlin, listen to me. You're okay. I need to ask you a few questions."

Her shock changed to embarrassment, her face blushing pink against the pale white of her skin. Shimmying out from under his grip, she bobbed her head. "Before I give a statement, I have to check on Warrior."

Slade stopped her from bolting by standing between her and the fussy dog. "Warrior will be fine for a few more minutes. Listen to me, okay?"

She exhaled, called a command to the animal, then glanced back at Slade. "You need a description?"

"Yes, but first what happened?" He scanned the perimeter of the practice yard and the parking lot. Nobody. But he heard doors opening in the distance and voices echoing out over the headquarters' parking lot. Maybe someone else had seen something.

Kaitlin glanced toward the sound of running feet. "I heard Warrior barking. He alerted me."

"I heard him, too," Slade said as he grasped her wrist. "Let's move toward the kennels so we don't get shot by one of our own."

She let him guide her until they were a few feet from Warrior's kennel. Then she pulled away and ran to the dog, her key ring jingling as she quickly opened the mesh-wire door.

Warrior bounded out, his frustrated whimpers echoing over the yard. The dog paced toward where Kaitlin had been snatched, then glanced up at his trainer.

"Sit. Stay."

The order wasn't as commanding as in the practice yard, but the dog did as Kaitlin said.

Slade saw two uniformed officers push around the building, guns drawn. He held up his hands. "Hey, over here. We had an intruder but…it's okay now."

As the officers gathered around, Slade explained what had gone down. "I exited my office and heard a K-9 officer barking. Someone tried to abduct Miss Mathers. He held a gun to her head, but she managed to get away. I pursued the attacker and called for him to halt. He refused and fired back. We both shot off a few rounds, but he managed to make it to the getaway car. Black, late-model van, old with a dent in the front passenger-side door. Temporary tag, smudged and unreadable. Vehicle headed west on Trapper Street. I got off a shot that hit the right back side of the van."

"We'll put out a BOLO."

Slade nodded on that.

"Get a good look at the attacker?" one of the officers asked.

Kaitlin spoke up. "He was wearing a dark mask like a ski mask. His eyes looked…so black, an eerie black. He must have been wearing special contacts because even the whites of his eyes looked dark."

Slade saw the shudder moving down her body. And felt the hair on his neck rising. This wasn't the first time he'd had a run-in with a man fitting that description. Last month, he'd glimpsed a masked gunman with blacked-out eyes fleeing Melody Zachary's hotel suite after a tense standoff that left K-9 detective Parker Adams with a gunshot wound. However, he didn't let on in front of Kaitlin that this suspect had to be the hooded man who'd been wreaking havoc on his entire department. The body count kept rising due to the heavy-handed work of a local crime syndicate run by a mastermind known as The Boss. And now someone within this criminal's organization had made a bold attempt right here on police grounds. Five months ago, his K-9 partner Rio had been stolen and now this. Someone was deliberately taunting him.

He wanted this case over and done with before someone else got killed.

Turning to the officer, he said, "That's an apt description. He was average height, maybe a hundred and seventy pounds, medium build. He wore black coveralls." Slade stopped, a shiver of familiarity moving down his spine. He shook it off, figuring things had happened so fast he still had a lot of images running through his head. Especially the one of Kaitlin being held a gunpoint.

"There was a wide silver zipper down the front," she added, her voice becoming stronger. "He had a…raspy voice. He kept telling me I had to go with him."

Kaitlin kept her hand on Warrior and petted the dog over and over. She was scared but was clearly putting on a brave front. Slade's heart still thumped against his chest. The image of that masked man holding her at gunpoint would stay with him for a long time.

After the officers took their statements and along with the crime scene unit, covered every inch of the area where the van had been idling, Slade finally told the others he needed to get Kaitlin home.

"I can drive myself," she insisted tersely, her pupils settling into a stubborn dark green. "Warrior always goes home with me. I'll be fine."

"I'm taking you home," Slade said in his best captain voice. "So don't argue with me."

She stared him down, then shrugged. "Then let's get out of here."

TWO

Word of the attack spread quickly.

Kaitlin's cell rang the minute Slade pulled the car into her driveway. The first call came from fellow trainer Harry Markham. "Kait, are you all right? I got a call from Callie."

"I'm fine," Kaitlin said, her eyes on Slade. The man was so solid and sure she couldn't help but feel safe, yet she worried that he'd take this kidnapping attempt to heart since he didn't take down the culprit. "It wasn't any fun, but I'm okay, really. Tell Callie—"

Her phone beeped another call. "That's Callie right now. I'd better talk to her."

She quickly told her supervisor, Callie Peterson, what had happened.

Slade got out and looked around her yard, then opened the car door for her.

"I'm home and Captain McNeal is here with me. He insisted on giving me a ride. Yes, I have Warrior. He warned me but...the masked man...he grabbed me from behind."

As she tightened her grip on the phone, Slade tightened his glare on her. "I have to go, Callie. Captain McNeal needs to get home to his family."

She hung up and let the next call, from her trainer friend Francine Loomis, go to voice mail. "They're all concerned," she told Slade. "We're all close. Like family."

"You left out the part where you tripped him up and jabbed him in the ribs. Or how you managed to kick that gun away like it was a soccer ball."

She blinked at the mention of her ordeal. "I went into automatic response, I think. Self-defense and officer training from years ago kicked in."

"You took a big risk. He could have killed you."

"He didn't. Because I knew you'd take him down before he ever reached that gun again."

His jaw hardened. "Yeah, well, I somehow managed to let him get away."

Was he implying that she had distracted him? Hard to say. The captain's expression was a study in frustration. But then, the man was hard to read on a good day. And this had not turned out to be a good day.

"You didn't let him get away. The perp was returning fire so you had to protect yourself."

He grunted, his silver-blue eyes doing an intimidating sweep of the neighborhood. When they reached her front door, he turned to her. "Give me your keys."

Kaitlin did as he asked, figuring it would save time and save her from arguing with him. The man was like a steamroller. He rolled right along doing his job without hesitation, but he sure didn't like to engage in chitchat. Slade McNeal was always focused and intent on getting the bad guys.

Except earlier, when he held me in his arms.

Or rather, when she'd clung to him like he was the last Kevlar vest and she had dibs. Looking at him now, seeing that coiled bundle of strength and determination in his body language, she tried to put the memory of his solid chest out of her mind. She'd think about Slade McNeal and his silvery eyes and quicksilver moods later when she was alone and couldn't sleep. It wasn't as if she hadn't thought of him before and often. Her heart went out to him and his little boy, Caleb.

Slade's wife had been killed two years ago in a car bomb that, according to word around the yard, had been intended for Slade. Then five months ago, his K-9 partner, a beautiful German shepherd named Rio, had been taken from his backyard. That attack had left his elderly father Patrick McNeal—a retired police officer—injured and in a coma for weeks. Top that with a five-year-old son who had withdrawn after his mother's horrible death.

No wonder the man was grumpy.

Slade opened the door and stepped through, one hand gesturing at her. "Stay behind me. We'll send Warrior in first."

She glanced back. "Good idea."

Kaitlin called the command and willed the still-green animal to do a good job. Since she was purposely training this particular canine officer to help find Rio, she wanted Warrior to impress Slade. The Belgian Malinois, eager to let go of some of his own pent-up energy, hurled past Slade and danced across the hardwood floors of the living room, his nose moving from the floor to the air.

"C'mon," Slade said, reaching behind to grab her hand.

His touch shot through Kaitlin like a sizzling dynamite fuse. She'd always had a little thing for the captain, but she wasn't so needy that she'd play this for all it was worth. If the man ever had a lightbulb moment and turned interested, she wanted him to come to her on better terms than her playing a damsel in distress.

She'd never be that woman. Not since the day she'd watched her mother being put in the ground. Kaitlin had learned the hard way to take care of herself. And she needed to remember that Captain McNeal was as tightly wound as a ticking clock. The man lived and breathed his job, especially since whoever had taken Rio kept coming after people they both knew.

He let her go once they were in the living room. "Kitchen looks safe."

She glanced across the hallway to her tiny efficiency kitchen. "It is, except for my cooking."

He almost smiled. "I'll take that under consideration."

Warrior rushed back, eager for a treat and a good rub-down.

"Didn't find anything, boy?" Slade asked, his tone softening toward the dog. He looked down at a basket by the door and found a chew rag, then held it out for Warrior. "He might have saved your life today."

Kaitlin went to her knees on the floor and tugged Warrior close, giving him a gentle hug. "Good boy. What a hero. Your barks warned me."

The captain looked really tall from this angle. "Yep. And what did you do? You walked right into a trap."

She stood so he wouldn't seem so intimidating. "I went around the building to see why Warrior was barking. I saw the van and thought someone might be lost or hurt. That's when the attacker came up behind me."

Slade didn't move a muscle, but she could see the throbbing pulse in his clenched jawline. "You could have called me."

"I really didn't have time to call anyone. Besides, I thought you were gone." She shrugged, tossing her ponytail. "You know what...I didn't even think, okay? I just acted on impulse, and I wasn't expecting any kind of danger."

He stepped back, his cold, blue gaze freezing its way around her tiny house. "Well, you need to think about it now. Whoever that was will probably be back. I don't think this was a random kidnapping attempt. They waited for the right moment and managed to get through a controlled gate to get to you."

Seeing the concern etched on his face, she said, "You're not making me feel very safe."

"You're not safe." He walked to the bay window in her living room. "Your attacker fit the same description of the man who's been harassing my whole team for months now. I'm pretty sure he or someone working with him is behind the recent string of attempted kidnappings we've had. And the string of murders we've racked up since the first of the year."

Shocked, she pushed at her hair. "Are you sure?"

"Yes. You said he had strange eyes, right?"

"Yes. They were all blacked out. Honestly, they didn't look real."

Slade seemed to go on alert after that comment. "They probably aren't real. He's using a mask and other methods to disguise himself."

"Why?" she asked, worried now that the crime syndicate might be targeting her. "Why would he come after me?"

He didn't answer her questions. "You might need protection 24/7."

Kaitlin almost laughed out loud. "Are you willing to do that?"

"I have to work on this case." He kept right on staring out the window. "But it might be a good idea to keep Warrior by your side at all times. And maybe you have a friend who can come and stay with you?"

"I won't endanger any of my friends," she said, shaking her head. "Warrior will do his job. That's what he's trained for."

"But is he ready?" Slade asked, staring down at the resting dog.

"He seemed ready today. We'll have to hope so," Kaitlin replied. "I'm not the type to live in fear, Captain McNeal."

He came close then, his face inches from hers. "And I'm not the type to let a woman think she's safe when it's obvious she's not, Miss Mathers." He stepped back. "Get your stuff. You and Warrior are coming to my house tonight."

Kaitlin couldn't believe the man. "No, we're not."

His tone brooked no argument. "Yes, you are." Then he held up his hand. "Look, I have a young son and my recovering father there. And two shifts of around-the-clock nurses. You won't be alone. *We* won't be alone."

Kaitlin thought it over, still reeling. "I don't want to impose on you."

"You won't be imposing. Caleb will be glad to see you. He's been asking about you...since the last time you babysat him. And it's just for tonight. Just until I can figure out the next piece of this puzzle."

Five-year-old Caleb had been traumatized when his mother had been killed in the car bomb. The quiet little boy suffered from nightmares and other issues. Kaitlin had worked a lot with Caleb, using her dogs to bring the boy out of his shell. But it had been a while since she'd seen him.

Wanting to understand what she'd be up against, she asked, "What do you know, Captain? About that man's creepy eyes?"

He hesitated, almost shut down. But she saw a flare of trust shifting through his expression. "I don't think they're his real eyes."

She let out a gasp. "Contacts? That's what I thought, too."

His nod was curt and quick. "I think so." His gaze moved over her, then he looked toward the big windows. "Call it a hunch, but I'd just feel a whole lot better if you'd come home with me."

"Isn't that highly unusual? I mean, do you always invite people in danger home with you?"

"No."

"Why start now?"

He took a step forward then stopped. "Because this case has me by the throat and…I'm almost certain your attempted kidnapping has something to do with this crime syndicate. I couldn't live with myself if…something happened to you." He inhaled, rubbed a hand down his face. "And…because you mean a lot to my son. He feels comfortable with you since you've babysat him a few times and allowed the trainee dogs to befriend him. Truth is, he's been through too much tragedy already…and he'd be devastated if something happened to you."

Kaitlin couldn't catch her next breath after that comment. "I can't stay at your house forever…"

"No, but I can keep you alive if you'll listen to me."

She couldn't argue with that. He'd scared her with his bold words and all this talk of a crime syndicate and a masked criminal. He'd scared her with that tormented need she'd seen hooding his eyes, too. He didn't want his little boy to suffer anymore.

However, going with Slade would be like stepping across that forbidden line she'd put up between them. She didn't like mixing emotions and business together. Things could get really messy.

But when she thought about that man's eyes, she got the shivers. And given the choice of staying here alone or being with Slade and his family…well, there wasn't a choice.

"I'll pack a bag," she said finally. Then she turned and hurried out of the room before she changed her mind.

Well, now he could add stupid to the list of traits he needed to refine. He had a feeling he'd regret bringing a woman home, kind of like sailors used to avoid having a female on their ship. Nothing good could come of it.

Slade looked around the big living room of the house he shared with his father and his son and a retired K-9 named Chief. The rambling craftsman home had plenty of room for one or two more. But it had been a long time since a woman, other than his father's team of home health care nurses and Caleb's after-school nanny, had stayed in this house for more than a few uncomfortable minutes—for what his daddy called a "casserole" visit. Single women and widows loved to bring them casseroles. The women all expected something in return, of course. A couple of them had even asked Slade to the monthly church social.

Slade couldn't oblige them. It made for awkward visits.

But hey, the food was good.

"She's pretty and nice," Patrick McNeal said. "Kind of different from most of the casserole girls."

Old Chief, retired and getting fat and sassy, lifted his head and sniffed the perfume in the air. Even the dog had noticed this feminine intrusion.

Slade turned from where he was making sandwiches and nodded at his father. "Pretty, nice and now…on some thug's hit list." He slapped ham between two slices of white bread. "Why would anyone go after Kaitlin Mathers?"

Papa, as Caleb liked to call him, ran a hand down his white-whiskered face. Still recovering from the injuries that had left him in a coma, he said, "Maybe they need a dog trainer."

Slade stopped the knife he'd aimed at the mayo jar. "Good point."

"You think this attack is connected to all the others? Whoever took Rio might need a qualified trainer, too."

"I'm betting it's related, for that reason and maybe

something more. I haven't come up with anything else, though."

Patrick held tight to his walker and turned to go back through the arched opening to his favorite chair in the den. Chief automatically followed him. "You'll figure it out, son."

Slade wondered about that. He and his dad didn't do much chitchatting here in the house. Caleb seemed to get agitated whenever they talked police business. But Patrick had made a connection that shouted at Slade. Someone might need Kaitlin's expertise. Or any of the trainers' expertise, for that matter. That someone obviously had taken Rio right out of the backyard. He'd have to beef up security around the training center. Not to mention keep a close watch on his son and his daddy. And he'd need to protect Kaitlin, whether she liked it or not.

Rubbing his hand on the back of his neck, he grunted at the twisted knots tightening his head and shoulders. Maybe he needed to hit the gym a little more to work out some of these kinks.

No, he just needed to catch The Boss. The mysterious leader of the local crime syndicate kept slipping through their fingers, but one way or another he vowed to bring this criminal to justice. Since the day his dog Rio had been taken right out of his yard and his father had been injured, he'd made this case a top priority. And his entire unit felt the same way.

He wanted his frail father to understand what he was trying to do.

He wanted his best K-9 partner back. Rio was part of his family.

He wanted his son to be strong and well and happy.

Then why don't you spend more time with the boy?

That question hit him hard in his gut. Patrick asked him

that at least twice a week. When he'd turned to Kaitlin in desperation after Rio's kidnapping, the dog trainer and his sometime-babysitter had hinted that it might help for him to take more time with Caleb. Maybe that was why he always got so befuddled and tongue-tied around the woman. Maybe that was why bringing her here wasn't such a good idea, after all. He didn't want the woman judging him.

She wasn't married and didn't have kids. But she sure had a way with animals and children. She was all honey and sweetness when she wasn't barking commands at K-9 dogs. Today, after things had settled down, her hair had shimmered like burnished gold in the light of early dusk, but her hazel eyes had remained cool and questioning each time her gaze landed on Slade. Except for that little bit of sympathy he'd seen there in shades of green and brown. The woman had been attacked and yet, she still felt sorry for him?

He didn't need anyone's pity.

Slade needed to be a better father, but…it was so hard to relate to his quiet, sad little boy. The boy missed his mother. And Slade felt the weight of guilt pressing like a two-ton chain on his shoulders. He and Angie had been fighting the day she'd died in that car bomb. His wife had been leaving him, probably for good, when she'd cranked the engine.

Slade endured the torment of causing her death each and every day. His daddy told him he should pray about his feelings, but Slade didn't think he was worthy of asking God to release him of this burden. That bomb had been meant for him. He shouldn't even be standing here. He couldn't look his own son in the eye.

And…he had the nagging suspicion that the bomb that had killed Angie was related to this current case. Especially since similar bomb threats had been found at Nicolette Johnson's former rental. Detective Jackson Worth and his K-9 partner, Titan, had found one bomb in the nick of time to save Nicolette. Her house had been damaged, but that only reinforced how much danger she'd been in to begin with.

Then Jackson had also been threatened with a bomb under his car. Titan, trained to detect explosives, had saved the day again.

They might not be so lucky next time. Too many killings and too many kidnapping attempts had everyone on edge. And after today's bold attempt, Slade was sure there would be a next time. His bones told him that something else was coming. He only wished he could figure out what.

THREE

Kaitlin had thrown her duffel bag in the spare bedroom, then immediately asked Slade if she and Warrior could go visit with Caleb. The little boy was in his room playing with his trains and trucks, according to Papa McNeal. Slade had nodded curtly, then returned to making some sort of dinner.

Now Kaitlin was watching closely while Warrior and Caleb got reacquainted.

"He's dif-fer-ent from Rio," Caleb said, the big word twisting up in his mind but sounding cute when he squinted through it. "And he's skinnier than Chief."

"Yes, he is," Kaitlin said. If she had to be forced to stay here tonight, at least she could visit with Caleb. "He's still young like you. But he likes little boys. And I've told him all about you."

Caleb's big blue eyes, so like his daddy's, widened. "He knows about me?"

"Of course," she said, her expression animated. "I told him he'd get to come and visit you soon. I'm still training him and you can help with that. I told him how smart you are and that you are very good with dogs. He needs to be gentle with children so you are the perfect person to help him learn."

Caleb tilted his head and gave her an impish stare. "Am I gentle?"

The innocent question tugged at Kaitlin's heart strings.

"Yes, you sure are. But you're also very brave. That's why I brought Warrior to visit with you."

Well, that and the fact that your domineering father told me in no uncertain terms that I would come here tonight.

She had Caleb for a distraction, at least. A good distraction. And she'd mostly given in to Slade's demand so she could see how Caleb was doing. She adored this little boy. He took her mind off what had happened today. He took her mind off the big man in the kitchen making sandwiches, the man who'd gruffed out an introduction when he'd brought her into the house.

"Papa, this is Kaitlin Mathers and her newest trainee, Warrior. You might remember her. She's visited Caleb and she's watched him for me at her place a couple of times. We had a prowler near the training yard who tried to kidnap Kaitlin. She's staying here tonight."

His father, white-haired and holding on to a walker, had smiled and nodded while Chief had hopped up to inspect Warrior. After the dogs had sniffed each other to their mutual satisfaction, Patrick McNeal had said, "C'mon in, Kaitlin. You'll be safe here."

She supposed law officers had their own code of speaking, because she was pretty sure she missed some of the undercurrents of that brief, curt conversation. She'd also heard bits of a whispered conversation when she'd come out of the bathroom.

Caleb didn't speak a lot, either, but tonight he'd actually talked to her more than the last time she'd seen him. That had been a few weeks ago when Slade had brought Caleb to work for a couple of hours and she'd offered to take him out onto the training yard. She'd promised Caleb they'd find his friend, but Slade hadn't asked her to talk to Caleb since then. And she'd tried to respect Slade's decision by not nagging him too much. She always asked about Caleb, though. Now she had a chance to help him again. She intended to keep that promise she'd made to the little boy, somehow. After the incident today, Kaitlin was once again reminded of how life could change in a minute. Something she'd learned after her mother had died.

Taking a quiet minute to thank God that she was safe and here now with this little boy, Kaitlin rubbed Warrior's soft fur, her gaze on Caleb. "So do you think you two can be friends?"

Caleb bobbed his head, his dark curls bouncing against his forehead. Then he reached up and patted Warrior on the head. "I can show him my secret hiding place. I wuv him."

"I do, too," Kaitlin said. She was about to ask Caleb where his hiding place was, but she looked up to find Slade standing at the door with a look of longing and regret on his face. His gaze slammed into hers with lightning-bolt precision, leaving her drained and shaky.

"Dinner's ready," he said. Then he turned and hightailed it back to the kitchen.

Wondering what was wrong with the man, and what was wrong with her for caring, Kaitlin gently tugged Caleb to his feet. "Let's go see what your daddy whipped up for dinner."

Slade ladled the vegetable soup the day nurse had made earlier into bowls to go along with the sandwiches. "Hope you like soup. Terri is a great cook. She let this simmer all day."

Not one for sparkling conversation, he decided to just give Kaitlin the soup and let her eat. After that scene in Caleb's room, he felt overwrought and disoriented. Truth was, seeing his son smiling and laughing with a pretty woman tore at the hole in his heart. He really should take one of the casserole girls up on attending the church social. Just to get out of the house more. Papa was always telling him he'd never find a woman if he didn't ever bother to be around available women. Why his dad worried about such stuff was beyond Slade.

Well, they both wanted Caleb to find a mother figure he could trust and love again. Slade didn't think he needed to be concerned about a female companion for himself, however. His job kept him occupied.

"Smells great," Kaitlin said. "Makes me think of my grandmother's kitchen."

"Where'd you grow up?" Papa McNeal asked, his hands pressed together.

"In Mesquite, just outside Dallas." She glanced at Caleb, then lowered her voice. "Just my mom and I, but my grandmother lived close by. My father had to…uh…leave when I was a baby and…my mother…passed away when I was a teenager. Then it was just Grandmother and me. But Grandmother had a sister here in Sagebrush, so after I left for college, she moved here to be closer to Aunt Tina. They both passed away just years apart."

Slade nodded, understanding she had chosen her words carefully because of Caleb.

"You all alone?" his son asked, clearly deciphering what "passed away" meant.

Slade hoped the boy didn't start asking about his mother. It was hard to explain over and over that she'd never come back to them.

Kaitlin glanced at Slade before answering. "I don't have any family nearby, but…I have Warrior and I have people I work with and go to church with. So no, I'm not alone."

Caleb's gaze moved from Kaitlin to Slade. "And you have us. Right, Dad?"

Slade felt as helpless as a new puppy. He grunted a reluctant, "Yeah, sure."

Warrior, having heard his name, did a little "Yeah, sure" of his own. That dog was a lot braver than Slade right now.

Papa, looking amused, took his soup from Slade and waited for him to sit down. Then he reached for Kaitlin's hand on one side and Caleb's hand on the other. "We say grace before our meals," he explained.

Kaitlin took his hand, then realized she'd have to take Slade's on her other side. She shot him a look that shouted "Oh, no."

So she was afraid of him? Maybe disgusted with him? She probably thought he was the world's worst parent. Or maybe the world's worst law-enforcement officer since he couldn't settle a five-month-long case.

He stretched his hand toward her, all the while preparing himself for the current of awareness he always felt when he was around her. Did she feel it, too?

She took his hand, then quickly lowered her head and shut her eyes.

Slade remembered having her in his arms earlier, remembered seeing that gun pointed at her temple, too. The first memory warmed his soul while the last one stopped him like a cold bullet.

He jerked his hand away before his daddy said Amen.

When he ventured a glance at the woman sitting at his kitchen table, he saw confusion and hurt in her pretty eyes.

Well, that was the effect he had on most women.

The house was quiet now.

Kaitlin lay on the comfortable bed in the spare room and listened, unable to sleep. Every creak settling in the walls, every twig brushing against the house, caused her to wake with a start. She hadn't tasted this kind of fear in a long, long time.

She thought about the man who'd brought her here. She should feel safe with him in the house and she did. But she couldn't get that masked man out of her head.

After dinner, Slade told her he had to finish up some paperwork. Mr. McNeal went to bed when his night nurse, Jasper, arrived. The big male nurse apparently slept in Mr. McNeal's room. Kaitlin, left sitting, offered to get Caleb ready for bed.

No one argued with her. She enjoyed helping Caleb with his bath and putting on his superhero pajamas. Then he insisted on showing her his favorite hiding place—a big plastic toy box that looked like a miniature house centered underneath the bay window in the dining room. Slade told her it was where Caleb and Chief apparently played and sometimes fell asleep. After demonstrating how he and Chief could both fit inside the little house, Caleb asked her to read to him. So she snuggled up against a Texas Rangers baseball pillow with Caleb and read several books. It wasn't long before Warrior joined them, content to curl up at Caleb's feet and stare with adoring eyes at his new friend.

A girl could sure get used to that.

But not this girl and not with this family. Slade McNeal practically shouted "Off limits" each time he looked at her. The man had pulled away from her during the dinner blessing. Did he find her that distasteful to touch? Did he wish he hadn't brought her into his house? Kaitlin had no answers. None at all. She knew how he'd made her feel earlier today when he'd comforted her after that attack… but she'd never know how Slade felt, good or bad. That man wore a coat of armor like a true knight. And he was good at rescuing damsels, no doubt.

But he needed to work on the Prince Charming factor a little more. Not that it mattered to Kaitlin. She'd given up on men a long time ago, since her work took up most of her time. She poured all of her love on the animals she trained. Maybe she was a lot more like Slade McNeal than she realized.

Now, wide awake and restless, Kaitlin got up and tugged her terry cloth robe over her flowered pajamas. Her throat burned like a parched desert. She needed a glass of water.

Opening the door slowly, so she wouldn't wake the whole house, she sent Warrior a command to stay. The big dog gave her a reluctant look, then curled back into a ball of fur.

Moonlight guided her up the wide hallway toward the kitchen. Remembering where Slade had put the glasses, Kaitlin found a juice glass in the cabinet and then ran some water from the sink. She quenched her thirst and turned to stare over at the big plastic storage box under the window.

And heard a definite clearing of someone's throat behind her.

Slade watched as Kaitlin pivoted, the glass in her hand, and stared out into the darkness. "Who's there?"

Hating the quiver in her voice, he pushed away from the rolltop desk in the corner of the den and stood. "It's me. Slade. I didn't mean to scare you."

He heard her inhale a breath. "You shouldn't sneak up on people like that."

"I didn't. I was sitting here in the quiet. I didn't know anyone else would be up."

She walked into the moonlight and his heart stopped.

Her hair was down and tumbling in a shimmering

honey-colored ribbon. Her robe was white but her pajamas had some sort of flower sprigs all over them. She looked young and vulnerable and beautiful.

But he didn't come out of the darkness to tell her that.

He couldn't move. He didn't know how to begin to flirt with a woman. He was old and bitter and washed up.

"What are you doing?" she asked. Then she drained the glass of water.

"Well, I was sitting here at my desk in my house, minding my own business."

"Then I'll leave you to it."

He stood up and caught her before she shot back up the hall. "Hey, are you all right?"

She looked down at his hand holding her wrist. "I thought I was. But…I keep seeing that man's eyes. I keep remembering that gun at my head."

Slade didn't stop to think. He tugged her close. "You've been through a bad experience. It's just nerves. You know you can talk to a counselor, right?"

She backed up and stared at him. "Yes, I know that. And that's very good advice."

He let her go. "You mean for myself, too, right?"

"And for Caleb. It might help."

"We've been that route," he said. "But when he's with you, he seems better." He didn't dare move any closer. "I've always wondered how you two bonded so fast, but I think I understand now. You lost your mother, too. What happened?"

A deep sigh shuddered through her. "She was a veterinarian and she was working late one night, sitting with a sick animal. A drug addict managed to talk his way in the back door. He attacked her with a surgical instrument after she didn't give him the kind of drugs he wanted. She bled to death right there on the floor."

Slade let out his own wobbly sigh. "Goodness. I had no idea."

"I don't talk about it much."

And Slade had specifically asked her to help his son. "I would have found someone else if I'd known—to talk to Caleb. I mean, it has to be hard for you—"

She backed up, shook her head. "I like being around him, letting him get to know the animals. I don't mind at all. Talking to him makes me feel better, and I just want to help."

"I know you do. And you're very persistent about such things."

She pushed at her hair, tugged at her robe. "*I* should just mind *my* own business."

He didn't agree with her, but he didn't encourage her, either. She was right. But he was glad she pushed at him. Somebody needed to hold him accountable. "I don't mind you helping Caleb. It's not that—"

"I'm going back to bed now."

Slade felt the rush of air as she moved away from him.

"Hey, wait a minute."

"You seem to want to be alone," she said, her voice a sweet whisper.

"Not tonight," he replied. "C'mon and sit with me awhile."

She stood there, hesitating. He could almost feel the conflicting thoughts rushing through her head. He felt the same kind of warning each time he was around the woman.

But she moved, finally. She went to the kitchen and put the glass in the sink and stood there for a minute staring out the window. Then she let out a gasp. "Slade?"

"What?"

"I—I think there's someone out there."

FOUR

Slade leaped into action.

Grabbing Kaitlin, he shoved her away from the window. "Stay inside."

He had his weapon drawn and was out the front door before Kaitlin could inhale. She stood in the shadows, fear and uncertainty clouding her mind until she took a deep breath. Hurrying down the hall, she called out to Warrior. "Come."

The dog trotted to her side, his tail wagging and his ears lifting. "C'mon, boy," she said, heading to the front door. She was about to open it and let the dog take the lead when the handle turned.

Backing up, Kaitlin held Warrior by his fur and quieted him. If the kidnapper had come back, she'd let Warrior deal with him this time. The canine sensed her apprehension. He let out a long, low growl.

The door opened and Slade walked in.

Kaitlin let out a sigh of relief and commanded Warrior to stay. "You're okay?"

"Yes." He gave Warrior a quick pat. "Someone ran away when I came out the door."

"Maybe I just imagined I saw someone. Warrior didn't alert."

"You didn't imagine anything. I heard them running and I found footprints in the dirt by the back fence. I think whoever it was hopped the fence and came right into the yard. You probably saw them before Warrior had time to pick up a scent."

"They know I'm here, then."

Slade moved closer. "Look, it could have been a kid out for thrills."

"Or it could have been that man again."

She shuddered in spite of the warm night. "I can't live like this. I won't live like this."

He reached for her, but she moved away, everything she'd held in check since being attacked pouring through her. "I had to live without a father. Don't even know where he is. And then I had to live without my mother. After hearing all the details of how she was murdered, I was afraid but I got over my fears." Her eyes brimmed with emotion. "I made myself get over all of it when I decided to become a police officer. I might not be a patrol officer anymore, but I learned how to protect myself...and I can still protect myself now. I won't let them win. I won't be afraid."

But she was afraid. Her worst nightmare had always been a fear of ending up just like her mother. She hated the fresh terror coursing through her. How could she control this? What should she do now? Would her prayers save her?

Slade pulled her toward him, his hands on her elbows. "It's gonna be all right. You don't need to worry. I'll put an officer on your house 24/7, I promise."

She backed away again. She couldn't depend on this man. She'd been independent for a long time now. "I have Warrior. I'm training him as an all-purpose so he can help you find Rio. And we'll find the man behind this, too."

Slade shook his head. "No, Kaitlin. There is no 'we' in this. You can't get involved. It's too dangerous."

"I'm already involved," she said, anger taking over her apprehension. "They're after me. I don't know why, but they want something from me."

"They need your expertise," Slade explained. "You know how to make Rio do his job. They don't. That means they want something or someone that they can't get to, and they need you and Rio to help them."

"So they'll just kidnap trainers and animals until they get what they want?"

She saw something there in his eyes, a flicker of uneasiness that surpassed the concern she'd already seen. "What are you thinking, Slade?"

"They're coming after *you* for a reason."

"You said because of my expertise."

"It's more than that, I think." He put his hands on his hips and exhaled slowly. "They must know that you and I are—that we're close. I mean, I came to you almost two years ago and asked you to help me with Caleb. You've been to our house before and you've had Caleb at your place when I needed a sitter. They've seen us together at the yard and…they've probably been watching you with Caleb at the park, walking down the block—"

Kaitlin gasped and put a hand to her mouth. "They wouldn't hurt *him,* would they? Slade?"

He hit his hand on the door frame. "I don't know. We have to consider every possibility."

A cold calm came over Kaitlin. She refused to give in to the dread that shadowed her like tattered black threads. And she surely wouldn't allow anything to happen to Caleb. "We have to consider that. If I'm around you and Caleb, then you both could be in danger."

He looked over at her. "You can't avoid us. You can't isolate yourself. We have to work through this together."

"But you just said I shouldn't get involved. You can't have it both ways."

"You're right, I can't. You're in danger and I need to come up with a way to protect you. But you're also good at your job. I need you to go about your normal routine. If you keep working with Warrior, we might be able to do something about this."

"Will you let me do that? Will you keep me informed and let me train Warrior to help?" She lifted her chin. "Don't shut me out, Slade. This is too important and I'm way too involved for you to go all stoic and righteous on me now."

A frown deepened his laugh lines. "Stoic and righteous? Is that how you see me?"

Kaitlin didn't want to pull any punches. "You're kind of single-minded and intense when it comes to this case. And I get that. Your partner went missing, your dad almost died and now your son might be a target." She held back a shudder. "You have every right to be on alert, Slade, but you need me. I want to help. If I don't, this fear will overcome me and I can't handle that."

He stood, silent and brooding, doubt flickering in his eyes. "You're right. I have a lot riding on this. My entire unit, for one thing. My job, my son. And you."

And you.

Awareness flashed through Kaitlin, a spine-tingling feeling that she couldn't deny. Did he feel it, too? This thing they had going? She wondered if she was just fixating on the one man who'd taken the time to get to know her over the years and had now possibly saved her life. Or maybe because Caleb was so adorable, she considered his daddy to be the same? No, this was about more than that.

They'd worked around each other for a couple of years now, but they'd both been professional and polite but standoffish. Then he'd approached her about using dog therapy to help Caleb out of his shell. And she'd readily agreed because she did empathize with the little guy since she'd been through something similar. And now they'd been thrown together in an intense brush with death. Being aware of Slade McNeal had gone up a notch or two from admiring him to admitting she was attracted to him.

Did he feel the same way? She decided that didn't matter right now. She only wanted Slade and his family to be safe. Caleb didn't need yet another trauma to deal with.

Slade McNeal was as strong as steel and as solid as an oak tree. The strands of silver near his temples matched that steely ice blue of his eyes. He was the kind of man she should run from, and fast. She needed to remember that, no matter the tension between them.

He must have realized what he'd said. "You are a part of this, Kaitlin. I can't let anything bad happen to one of our best trainers."

She'd take that, for now.

"Then let me help you. I'm trained to teach K-9 dogs on how to be the best. I know all the rules and I know all the procedures and precautions. And even though I quit the force, I'm experienced in all kinds of self-defense courses."

He nodded, a curt, quick movement. "We'll need to put surveillance on your house and the training yard. You can't be alone. You'll need someone at work with you at all times and you might need to stay with someone for a while. I can put Melody on this. She's as caught up in this case as the rest of us."

"Melody Zachary?" Kaitlin knew Melody. She was a good cop and a great friend who'd recently helped solve her nephew Daniel's murder. "But she's engaged now. She's busy planning her wedding to Parker."

"Yep, that seems to be going around a lot these days, but she still has a job to do. You can help her with the wedding stuff. You women seem to love that kind of thing."

Figuring he wasn't the marrying type, she said, "We all have a job to do." Then her smile broke. "But it would be fun to help plan a wedding."

Slade nodded. "I guess that's a win-win." He took another breath. "Look, it's late. We've got a lot to contend with. Think you can get some sleep?"

"I don't know. I'm exhausted but wired. I'll try."

He motioned to Warrior. "Take him and go back to bed."

"What about you?"

"I don't sleep."

The next morning, Slade was back in his office bright and early. He'd dropped Kaitlin by her house to get a few things, then they'd driven in together. The other trainers had been briefed on what happened yesterday, so they knew to stay on high alert. Slade had reported to the chief and now he was about to brief his unit and bring everyone up-to-date. They'd have to retrace their steps yet again to see what they'd been missing.

But when he turned to stare at the big white board where he'd placed all the clues and details they'd managed to collect over the past few months, he couldn't help but scan the pieces of the puzzle one more time.

His father had been attacked and Rio had been kidnapped. Eva Billow's son Brady had then been taken because the kid had witnessed the attack. Austin Black and his bloodhound Justice had found the child. And Austin had found love with the boy's pretty mother Eva. At least they'd gotten one arrest out of that part of the case. Only that lowlife Don Frist wasn't talking. Nobody wanted to talk, not even Charles Ritter, the high-powered lawyer Don Frist had ratted out. Ritter was sitting in jail. Which meant The Boss was a very powerful and dangerous man.

Then two more thugs had been murdered, and two middle management members of the crime syndicate were also dead. He stared at the mug shots of Andrew Garry, aka Blood, and Adrianna Munson, aka Serpent. They were all snakes in the grass in Slade's mind. Next up, Gunther Lamont—the Businessman—allegedly the second in command, now dead. Shot by Ski Mask Man. And last but certainly not least, dirty cop Jim Wheaton—who'd been on the syndicate's payroll—had been taken down by the cops during a hostage crisis.

They were getting closer and closer to The Boss. Slade should thank the man for culling his own criminals to the point of having no one to trust. That made a man desperate and dangerous. The Boss would slip up and when he did, Slade planned to be there to catch him. Trying to kidnap Kaitlin in the training yard and sending a thug to his house last night made this even more personal for Slade. The Boss kept toying with all of them, but he would slip up soon and Slade would be ready and waiting.

As he stood there going over everything in his head, he realized this had always been personal. They'd taken Rio out of *his* yard and tried to kill *his* father. And come to think of it, each of his team members had come dangerously close to getting killed, too. But all roads always came back to Slade and his family. Starting with Angie dying in that car bomb two years ago.

As the entire Special Operations K-9 Unit filed in, one by one, Slade nodded and spoke to each. Austin Black and Lee Calloway talked to each other as they headed to the coffeepot.

Valerie Salgado, a rookie who'd more than earned her stripes, laughed at something Jackson Worth said. And one of Slade's best friends, Parker Adams, nodded to Slade.

"What's up?" Slade asked when Parker came up to him.

"Can we talk later?" Parker asked. "I need to run something by you."

"Sure," Slade replied, curious. "Lunch after the meeting?"

"That'll work," Parker said. "Melody might be able to make lunch." He nodded and took a seat.

Wondering what that was all about, Slade started the meeting. "I know you've all been briefed on what transpired yesterday behind the training yard. Trainer Kaitlin Mathers's attempted kidnapping is now considered part of this case. Ski Mask Man has struck again."

Everyone started mumbling and talking. Slade held up a hand. "We're gonna go over every inch of evidence we have and we're going to pursue every lead. We want Rio back, but more than that, we want our town back. So let's start at the beginning."

The team had interviewed a low-level snitch named Pauly Keevers and all he'd told them was that there was something buried in the Lost Woods, a heavily wooded forest on the edge of town that hid a multitude of crime and evil. Pauly was dead now, too, taken out by the syndicate. Then informant Ned Adams was found buried in the woods.

"It looks like The Boss is killing people so they won't talk."

Jackson Worth spoke up. "Not to mention the infamous code we've tried to break and Daniel Jones's grave being dug up. And we did find that brick of cocaine. But two or so pounds of cocaine wouldn't bring about this much crime."

Not long after setting up surveillance in the Lost Woods, Parker Adams and his K-9 partner Sherlock had helped Slade find a small amount of cocaine, heavily scented to disguise it, in the woods.

Slade went back over that find. "You're right about that, Worth. It wasn't enough to cause this amount of secrecy and criminal intent. I believe there must be something else buried out in those woods."

"A body, maybe?" someone suggested.

Slade nodded. "That…or something worth much more than that small amount of cocaine we found."

Jackson spoke again. "Makes sense that we need to keep searching. They dug up that kid's grave, but they're still looking, too."

"Agreed, but we have to be careful," Slade replied. "The chief has given us special permission to stay on top of this, but let's keep in mind we have to continue to follow procedure and the chain of command."

Everyone nodded on that.

Parker again reported on how Detective Melody Zachary had solved part of a cold case that involved her sister Sierra and her nephew Daniel Jones. She'd found evidence that proved Jim Wheaton had killed Daniel and that her sister had not committed suicide. She'd been murdered. Did it all tie back to this case?

"No answers there. Dead men—and women—tell no tales," Parker said.

The body count kept rising. And so did Slade's blood pressure.

"Let's go back to that cocaine find," Slade said, a nagging feeling centered in his gut. "It wasn't enough to create this kind of violence."

"More like a smoke screen," Jackson said. "There has to be something else, something bigger out there."

"We'll have to find a reason to have another look," Slade replied, jotting notes on the board. "We'll set up more surveillance, too."

He believed the answers to this case were buried somewhere in those woods. He also believed that one of their highly trained K-9 officers would help him find whatever or whoever was out there. Now Kaitlin was training Warrior as just such a K-9.

"This brings us to Kaitlin Mathers. We're pretty sure they have Rio, but why try to kidnap a trainer?"

Valerie Salgado raised her hand. "Because they know she's smart and capable of handling a dog and they know she's been involved with you and your son. Hit us where it'll hurt."

Slade nodded. "I'm afraid that's it. Which means we have to put a tail on Kaitlin 24/7, for her own protection. And hopefully to find a pattern—someone following her, watching her. She'll go about her business and continue to train Warrior."

"I'll be glad to help with surveillance," Valerie offered. "And I don't mind hanging with Kaitlin."

They talked some more about recent events.

Then Slade stated the obvious. "I think Ski Mask Man might be more than your basic low-level thug." He glanced around the room then wrote on the board. "The Boss? Is he Ski Mask Man?"

While everyone chewed on that, Slade took one more sweeping look at the pictures and notes on the board.

"I'm pretty sure this whole setup has been aimed at me." He went back over the facts again, starting with the car bomb. "The Boss wants something that's buried in those woods, but he wants to make me suffer until he finds it. He's getting desperate, and that means we're all in jeopardy. So be on the alert at all times. We can't rest right now. It's too dangerous."

After everyone filed out, Slade turned to stare at the board again. Who was The Boss? And when would he make his next move?

FIVE

Slade went into the diner on the outskirts of town, still wondering why Parker and Melody couldn't talk to him at the office. Maybe Parker had a lead but was afraid to share it with the whole class. After the Jim Wheaton incident, Slade could certainly understand that. It was hard to trust anyone these days, but his gut told him he could trust all the members of his unit, especially Parker Adams. If Parker had something he only wanted to share with Slade, then that was all right by Slade.

He checked on Kaitlin before leaving for the lunch meeting. He found her hard at work out in the noonday heat, sending Warrior through all the obstacle courses and training runs.

Slade made a point to make sure she wasn't alone. Francine Loomis waved at him, her short dreadlocks lifting around her face, her smile always positive and uplifting. She'd watch out for her friend Kaitlin, no doubt there.

"Still putting him through his paces, I see."

Kaitlin turned at the sound of his voice, her expression cautious. "That's my job."

"How you feeling today?"

"I'm fine." When he didn't respond, she added, "I'm okay, Slade. Back to work. Work always helps calm me."

"You'll have an escort home and you'll have a car out front all night."

She nodded and sent Warrior for another practice run. "And I have Warrior. I think he gained more experience yesterday than he could have in a week."

"He wasn't practicing yesterday. He alerted us to you being in danger. That's the sign of a good officer."

"I want him to be good. Like everyone around here, I want this case solved. Warrior can help with that, I hope."

"We'll stay on it." He turned to leave. "I'm headed to lunch." Then he pivoted. "Oh, Kaitlin, I thought maybe you could come by and visit again with Caleb, maybe bring Warrior, too. He really took a shine to that dog."

She looked worried. "Do you think that's wise? I don't want to put Caleb in any danger."

"You'll be with me, too." He looked off into the distance. "Of course, these thugs did kidnap Rio right out of my yard."

"I guess we're not safe anywhere," she replied.

Frustrated, Slade nodded. "We'll stay close and keep an eye out, but yes, come to our house. Maybe have lunch with us?"

She hesitated, her expression guarded. "Okay. I'd like that. How 'bout Saturday? I don't have much planned then."

"We'll see you then. And in the meantime, be alert and stay safe."

He scanned the practice yard and the surrounding street before leaving. The back gate had been reinforced, too. Whoever had managed to slip in last time would find it hard to get in now. Everyone at headquarters had been alerted to be on the lookout for that black van, but Slade figured it was hidden in a warehouse somewhere. He wished he could find it. There were hundreds of black utility vans around the area. He could have the crime scene unit pull up makes and models. That might jar something loose.

Now he sat in the Sagebrush Diner wondering how he was supposed to keep his family and Kaitlin safe. When the door swung open, he waved to Parker and Melody, still wondering what they had to tell him. They'd already been through a lot together. Melody had been taken by Ski Mask Man and Parker had been shot by the thug when he came to Melody's rescue. Melody had matched up a cheap watch that had belonged to Daniel as containing the mysterious code the bad guy wanted. Ski Mask Man had taken the watch and while he'd gotten away yet again, thankfully Parker had saved Melody from a worse fate. The pretty, focused detective would make a good match for Parker.

Slade figured a man needed that kind of woman in his life. He thought about Kaitlin and wondered about the rest of her story. She'd obviously lost out on some things. They had that in common.

"Thanks for meeting with us," Parker said.

"No problem." Slade stood and greeted Melody. "Good to see you."

A waitress materialized and told them the special of the day. After they'd ordered their food, Parker glanced around, then looked back at Slade. "Melody has a theory and...we need you to hear her out."

"I'm listening," Slade replied.

Melody took a sip of her water, then let out a sigh. "I think I might know who Daniel's father is, and I wanted to meet with you to ask you about obtaining some DNA to prove it."

Now Slade was really listening. "Okay, but who and why me?"

Parker took Melody's hand. "We think it's your friend Dante Frears."

Slade put down his coffee cup. "What? He's happily married with a toddler. I must be missing something."

Parker nodded. "He wasn't always married. We think he had an affair with Melody's sister Sierra. When you get back to work, take a long look at Daniel's picture."

Melody gave Slade a beseeching glance. "I have one right here." She took the wallet-size print out of her purse and handed it to Slade. "I saw it right away when I encountered Frears at the Founders Ball last month. Their eyes—that pale silvery-blue color is distinctive, and they both have almond-shaped eyes, too."

While the kid did bear a resemblance to Dante, that didn't mean they were father and son. "Is this all you've got?"

Melody put the picture away and continued. "I've thought about it a lot. Frears is wealthy and more than able to support a child. My sister had someone taking care of her but she wouldn't tell anyone who—not even me. Daniel's girlfriend, Allie, says she thinks a rich man had an affair with my sister. She said Daniel knew his father but wouldn't talk about it. She thinks they had some sort of falling out…right before Daniel was shot."

Slade didn't want to buy into this, but Parker and Melody were both savvy police officers. He owed it to them to listen, at least. "But why Dante? He's a pillar of the community, a decorated veteran. He gave that huge donation to help us find Rio. He's always been behind the Sagebrush K-9 division."

"And all of that is good and fine," Parker said. "We just need you to get some of his DNA and let us test it—just so Melody can know the truth. If it was your son or nephew, you'd want to know, right?"

Slade couldn't argue with that. "Yes, I would. But I can't just march up to my best friend and ask him to hand over his DNA."

Parker glanced at Melody. She took a breath and said, "No, but you get invited to a lot of his fancy parties. It'd be easy for you to find a way to get his DNA."

Slade couldn't believe what they were asking him to do. "So you want me to go to his home and sneak around and do this? Without a warrant? Without probable cause? What if you're wrong?"

"Then I'll drop it," Melody promised. She motioned to Parker.

He leaned close. "Captain McNeal, if you consider what this means, you might be able to solve this case."

Slade's head shot up. "Come again?"

Parker tapped a finger on the table. "If Dante was Daniel's father, could he be retaliating for Daniel's death? You got blamed for it, but we now know Jim Wheaton made the kill shot. Frears might not know that or care. But if he does, then that's motive to come after our unit and especially you. It makes sense that someone with a lot of money is behind all of this."

"Someone who is also desperate and determined," Slade added, thinking Dante had no reason to be desperate. The man ran a legitimate corporation that involved several different investments—real estate and financing being at the top. He owned a lot of companies around town, too. Would his friend use one of those corporations or one of his businesses to hide a criminal empire? Could one of those companies have a fleet of black vans?

Slade couldn't see it. Or maybe he didn't want to see it. He sat silent while the waitress brought their blue-plate specials. Outside, the June sunshine sizzled in heat waves while Slade's mind hissed a warning that he couldn't voice.

They couldn't be right. Dante was a decorated soldier. He'd saved Slade's life more than once when they'd served together. But he was also a demolition expert. The man knew all about explosives—how to make them and how to detonate them. Dante handled C-4 the way a toddler handled Play-Doh. Slade had certainly seen that with his own eyes on the battlefield. But that didn't mean Dante had planted that bomb in Slade's car, did it?

He stared at Parker. "This is a bit far-fetched, don't you think?"

"You got any better ideas?" the detective asked.

Slade chewed on that while he tried to enjoy his chicken-fried steak. "No, I don't." He stared at his plate for a minute then said, "I'll see what I can do. But not a word to anyone until I can prove or disprove your theory. And even if I do, we can't use it in court."

Melody gave her fiancé a quick glance full of relief. "We haven't said anything about this. We wanted to talk to you first. The man's your best friend. I'd like to be wrong on this, but I don't think I am." She cleared her throat. "I don't want to press charges or anything like that so we won't need to use the DNA as evidence right now. I just need answers as to why Daniel was shot and why my sister died."

Slade lifted his head again. "You've already established she didn't commit suicide. You don't think Dante had anything to do with her death, too, do you?"

When Melody didn't answer, Slade dropped his fork. "I can't see Dante killing a woman in cold blood, especially the possible mother of his son. I'm sorry, but I can't go for that scenario."

Parker lowered his voice. "If he's The Boss, he'd be willing to kill anybody who stands in his way, don't you think?"

Images of the man holding Kaitlin at gunpoint yesterday

hissed through Slade's mind. Someone was sure willing to do desperate things. But Dante? It didn't make sense.

But Slade remembered one thing about yesterday's attempted kidnapping. That man had every opportunity to put a bullet through Slade and Kaitlin. What had stopped him?

I could have shot him easily, too, Slade thought. He'd hesitated because of Kaitlin. And because he wanted to bring the man in alive so he could get some answers. Now he only had more questions.

Slade had lost his appetite. "I'll have to think long and hard on this." He glanced from Parker to Melody. "I'll go back over everything and I'll consider what you've told me here today. I'll let y'all know if I get any leads on this."

"We know he's your friend," Melody said, "but…we also figure that gives him an almost perfect cover, too."

Slade inclined his head. "Because he'd have an in to our department. No one would suspect our biggest benefactor of double-crossing us."

"Exactly," Parker said. "I'm sorry, Captain, but this could be the missing part of the puzzle."

Slade paid for their meal, then turned back to the two detectives sitting with him. "If what you're telling me is correct, then I've been the biggest fool of all time."

"It's not your fault," Melody said, her tone sympathetic. "He fooled all of us. Especially my sister."

"Allegedly," Parker whispered. "We don't have any proof yet."

"You will," Slade replied, making his decision. "I intend to get that DNA, one way or another, and I'm hoping to be able to prove you wrong."

Kaitlin hated this. She'd turned around a hundred times today, wondering if someone was out there watching her.

Someone who might spring on her again and try to kidnap her.

And why? So she could bark orders at Rio? So whoever had the K-9 officer and the trainer would be able to use both of them for something illegal? It didn't make any sense to her at all. Rio had been missing for five long months now. Would he remember the commands they'd taught him? Would he remember her or Captain McNeal?

She thought back over her earlier conversation with Slade. Good thing she'd learned captain-speak over the years. The man mostly grunted out orders and commands, but rarely just came out and asked for help. She was touched as well as confused about his request that she come back to his house this weekend and visit with Caleb. But then, the captain loved his little boy even if he didn't have a clue as to how to deal with Caleb's silent moods and nightmares. Plus, she knew the other reason McNeal wanted her close. He felt responsible for her. The man took the world onto his broad shoulders and now she was one more thing to add to his list of concerns.

"What are you thinking about so hard?" Francine asked, her finger poking at Kaitlin's rib.

Kaitlin shook her head. "Life in general. I don't like this feeling of being unsafe. I'm beginning to doubt everyone around here."

The other trainer slanted her head and stared at Kaitlin with big brown eyes. "You know you can trust me, don't you?"

"Of course."

"Good then, 'cause I'm on you like white on rice." She giggled and winked at Kaitlin.

Kaitlin smiled at her always optimistic friend. "I happen to love rice and I happen to consider you my best friend, so I'm good with that."

"And I get to be your roomie for a few days. My mama is so thrilled that you and Warrior are gonna be staying with us this weekend."

"Could be a lot of weekends between staying with you and having Valerie or Melody staying with me on some weekdays," Kaitlin retorted. "Your mom might decide she's tired of us by then."

"Nah, she loves you. And besides, I think Captain Mc-Neal is gonna crack this case soon. Whoever tried to take you made one fatal mistake. They came onto our territory. No one around here will stand for that."

"I hope you're right," Kaitlin said. "And I hope Mc-Neal does find the culprit. I don't intend to live like this the rest of my life."

She'd only agreed to go to Francine's house later this week so they could both work on training Warrior. It would be good to put him in a different environment and see how he operated. And she always had fun when she was with Francine. Her friend had a big, loving family that had embraced Kaitlin the first time she'd gone with Francine to Sunday dinner. She loved being with them.

"I'm blessed to have you watching my back," she said.

Francine lifted a dark eyebrow. "You got the captain looking out for you now, girl. The way he looked at you this morning, I'd say you got more than that."

Kaitlin slanted her head. "Excuse me?"

Francine twirled one of her tiny braids. "I think Captain has his eye on you. In a good way."

Kaitlin ignored the thread of awareness that moved down her spine. "You're crazy, you know?"

"I've been told that. But I'm also very observant. I see what I see and I see a lot."

"You also talk in riddles."

"But I speak the truth."

Kaitlin laughed at her friend's antics. She could always depend on Francine to be the comic relief, even when she was brutally honest.

"We'll see about that," Kaitlin said. "I'm going over to his house on Saturday."

"Uh-huh."

"To spend some time with Caleb."

"Uh-huh."

She shook her head. "Don't go getting any ideas."

"Whatever you say." Francine grinned, then went back to her paperwork.

Kaitlin didn't tell her friend she was beginning to get some ideas of her own. Captain McNeal was good-looking and intense. Hard not to notice that. Hard not to be attracted to that. But…she didn't want to go down that road. The man lived for his work and from what she'd heard around the precinct, he didn't have time for any kind of personal relationship.

And neither did she. Kaitlin had learned a long time ago that she could only depend on herself. Even when someone was threatening her. When it came right down to it, she might have to take matters into her own hands. In order to survive.

SIX

Kaitlin checked all the windows and doors one more time. Locked tight. Then she lifted a panel on one of the wooden blinds in her living room and saw the patrol car parked out past the streetlight. Someone was watching over her out there and Valerie was asleep in the guest room.

Warrior was nearby, too. The dog would alert at the least bit of noise. She could rest easy for now.

Her cell rang, making her jump. Hating this skittishness, she took a deep breath and answered. “Hello.”

“Kaitlin, it’s Slade McNeal.”

As if she didn’t recognize that curt, gravelly voice.

“Hello, Captain. Yes, I’ve checked the windows. Yes, the cruiser is parked outside and Valerie is sleeping here tonight. And yes, Warrior is right beside me.”

“Can I speak now?” Slade asked, waiting.

She swallowed hard. “I guess so. What did you need to say?”

“Well, now that I think about it, you did answer all my questions. Are you sure you’re okay, though?”

“I just told you, yes.” She didn’t want to sound ungrateful. “I’m okay, Slade, really. A little jittery, but then I’ve never come close to being abducted before so my new normal is a bit shaky right now.”

"I could come over, sit with you until you get sleepy."

Kaitlin considered that offer and thought about having him here in her house, sitting on her couch. Tempting, mighty tempting. "I'm a big girl. I can take care of myself."

"These people are dangerous, Kaitlin."

"I know that. I'm the one who had a gun pressed to her temple, remember?" And now she had her own pistol loaded and nearby.

"I can't forget," he rasped out. "Okay, do it your way but be cautious. Put my number on speed dial."

She could do that, but she wouldn't need to. "I will, I promise. Now you try to get some sleep, too."

"I don't sleep," he said, probably to remind her again.

"Right." She wished him a good night and ended the call. Then she looked down at Warrior. "Neither will I, but he doesn't need to know that, does he?"

Slade put down the book he'd finished reading to his son. "Time to get some shut-eye, okay?"

Caleb looked up at him with big blue eyes. "I like Warrior."

Slade leaned forward in his chair. "I like Warrior, too. He's a loyal officer."

Caleb's eyelids became droopy. "Want Rio back."

"Me, too," Slade replied. He leaned forward and stood, his hand touching on his son's dark curls. "Sleep tight."

"No bed bugs bite," Caleb said in a sleepy whisper.

"No bed bugs bite," Slade repeated, wishing he could keep all the bad things in life away from his son.

But…that wasn't possible. Caleb had lost his mom in a horrible way and even though the little boy didn't witness the explosion, he'd certainly heard and seen enough to realize that his mother wasn't coming back. The same with Rio. How many hits could one kid take before he shut down completely?

Thinking about Kaitlin and how good she was with Caleb, Slade walked into his little corner office in the big den and sank down in the worn leather chair behind the battered desk.

What was it about this woman that always had him on edge?

She wasn't a classic beauty but she had nice honey-colored hair and those pretty, catlike hazel eyes. She was what his deceased mom would have called fresh-faced and earthy. Not a lot of fancy makeup or jewelry. Kaitlin's beauty shined from within. Maybe because she was a devout Christian.

Slade shook his head at that, thinking he was more of a doubting Christian. He certainly didn't shine very much. He shuffled through the papers on his desk, and wondered for the hundredth time how he could protect all the people he cared about.

Including Kaitlin Mathers.

Of course he cared about the woman. He cared about all the K-9 trainers. They were a vital part of his department. But Kaitlin, well, she'd always been there, willing to help with Caleb, willing to go the extra mile to make the animals do the best job possible. Now she was hard at work training Warrior. He'd be a good all-purpose officer. The best.

Slade sat up, his mind whirling. What if the syndicate came after Warrior, too? How long could he fight off these people? Then he thought about Melody's accusations against Dante Frears.

That put a whole new wrinkle on this troubling case.

And gave Slade a whole new set of worries to mull over.

Maybe he did need to turn back to God. Because he

prayed he wouldn't have to take down a man who'd been his friend for most of his life. He prayed that Melody and Parker were wrong.

But in his heart, in his gut, he had that feeling of aching emptiness and nagging irritation. What if they were right?

Kaitlin woke up and stared at the clock. Three in the morning. Her mother used to call this the loneliest hour. A shudder moved down Kaitlin's spine. Had she dreamed about her mother? She thought so, but her mind refused to go back into that dream. She had a vague flash of her mother, smiling at her, laughing, reaching out a hand.

"Are you trying to warn me, Mama?"

Warrior heard her speak and stirred from his doggie bed at the foot of her bed. The big dog whimpered a greeting and waited for her to pat him.

Kaitlin rolled off the bed and grabbed her robe. "Let's make rounds," she said, giving Warrior a command.

Together, they moved up the hallway, the night-light she kept there glowing enough to show the way to the kitchen and living room at the front of the small house. After passing Valerie's closed door, Kaitlin automatically went to a window to check for the cruiser. It was still there, parked in front of her house.

"Good. We're safe for now."

She refreshed Warrior's water and set the big bowl down, then went to the sink to get herself a drink. Sipping her water, she thought about last night while she'd been in Slade's house. If she hadn't seen that shadow out the window, they might have sat and talked well into the night.

And she might have gained some insight into the man's head and heart. Did she really want to go there? Warnings sparked through her mind like a fuse sparking toward dynamite. She'd worked with men like Slade McNeal for most of her adult life.

No, that wasn't exactly true. She'd worked with a lot of uptight, hardheaded police officers, but she'd never been around a man like Slade before. He was uptight and hardheaded and most people considered him hard-hearted, too. But she'd seen the good side of the man. He loved his son, but he was afraid of what his work had done to Caleb. Slade had swallowed his pride by reaching out to her for help. That gesture showed Kaitlin a lot of things about him. He cared enough to put his own feelings aside. He had a heart, but he'd built that proverbial wall around it to protect himself in the same way he tried to protect everyone else.

Including her, now.

"I can't do this," she whispered to herself. "I can't let my feelings go beyond helping Caleb." If she got all caught up in trying to save Slade McNeal, she'd be the one who wound up hurt. Not to mention how awkward that would make things around the training yard.

"Not a good idea," she said, looking down at Warrior. The dog woofed a reply, then looked around for something to sniff.

And found it by her front door.

Kaitlin's gaze followed Warrior. The dog stopped and ran his nose along something shining white lying on her hardwood floor. Her pulse skittering, Kaitlin hurried toward Warrior. "What you got there, boy?"

Warrior looked up at her with eager eyes, then sniffed the piece of paper again.

Kaitlin went back to the kitchen and grabbed a set of tongs from the big container of utensils she kept on the counter. "Let's see what that is." She carefully lifted the paper, holding it tight with the tongs until she got it over to the counter where the stove light cast out enough light for her to see.

The words printed on the paper caused her to gasp and step back shivering.

I'm watching you.

Kaitlin turned, her back pressed against the counter, her heart pumping so loudly she could hear it over her erratic breathing. The house was dark and quiet, but she strained to hear anything else that might signal danger. Should she go to the window and check for the cruiser? Should she go back to her bedroom and get her gun and her phone? Or maybe let Warrior out to do a search around her house?

"No," she whispered, swallowing her fear as she hurried to Valerie's room. "That's what they want me to do."

She stood at the door, her eyes adjusting to the shadows as she strained to hear the sounds of the creaking house, the wind causing a branch to tap against the window.

Slowly, she calmed herself enough to think straight. Someone had managed to get to her porch and slip this note underneath her door. Even with a cruiser parked outside. Even with a trained K-9 officer present in her house.

"Who are you?" she asked out loud. Then she knocked on Valerie's door.

Valerie was up and at the door, her weapon held down by her side. "What's wrong?"

Warrior whimpered and woofed, probably sensing Kaitlin's anxiety. The dog badly wanted to get on with things.

"Someone slid a warning note under my front door." She motioned to Valerie to come up the hall and then showed her the note.

Warrior went to the door and sniffed again, then whimpered.

"Not now, Warrior," she said, calling him over. She put her hand on a tuft of his fur. "Not tonight, boy. They want me to let you out there. But I'm not going to let them win tonight."

Valerie readied her weapon, her green eyes flaring bright. "They don't know I'm here. I'm going out there."

"You need backup," Kaitlin said, following the female officer around the windows. Valerie had left her K-9 partner Lexi kenneled with another handler, but now Kaitlin wondered if the apprehension-trained dog should have come along, too. "Don't go until I call someone."

Valerie kept moving. "Hurry, then."

Kaitlin rushed back to her room and got her cell and her pistol. She could alert the cruiser at least. The officer had given her his cell number earlier in the evening.

Kaitlin punched in the numbers and waited.

But no one answered.

Slade heard the buzzing of his phone and came wide awake to grab it off the nightstand. "McNeal."

"Sir, it's Pete Ross."

The patrolman assigned to watch Kaitlin.

Slade was up and searching for his clothes. "What is it?"

"I saw someone up on Miss Mathers's porch. I'm doing a walk around the perimeter of the yard. I think he came through the back gate."

Slade closed his eyes and let out a grunt. "I'm on my way."

Dressing quickly, he alerted his dad's night nurse that he'd been called to work. The male nurse was used to this so he replied okay and went back to his recliner in Papa's room. He was good at listening for Caleb, too.

Slade was out the door and in his car in minutes. He was turning the corner to Kaitlin's street when his cell rang. It was Kaitlin.

"I hate to bother you, but Officer Ross isn't responding to my calls."

Slade turned into her driveway. "He called me. I'm in your driveway now."

"Oh, what a relief."

Slade wasn't sure if she meant him being here or if she was just glad the officer guarding her was alive and well.

He took the steps and was knocking at her door in seconds.

Kaitlin opened the door and looked past him, Valerie behind her. "Where is Officer Ross?"

"He's making rounds in your backyard. He saw a prowler."

Valerie pushed past them. "I didn't see him anywhere. I'll go check it out."

Kaitlin shut the door and turned to Slade. "That must be why he didn't answer my calls."

"How many times did you try to call him?"

Sighing, she held her hands against her robe. "Several times, and so did Valerie. He didn't answer so I got worried."

"Maybe he put his phone on silent to do a search," Slade replied. "That's probably why he called me."

"I'm glad he did." She pushed at her long hair. "I mean, I thought maybe I was imagining things but...whoever was out there left me a message under my door."

"What?" Anger and frustration snaked through Slade. "Let me see."

She took him to the counter and pointed to the note.

I'm watching you.

Slade stared at the scrawled black words that stood out from the crisp white paper, a chill hardening his spine.

Kaitlin's voice was low and gravelly. "I think they expected me to send Warrior out to investigate. I didn't. I figure if I had, he wouldn't have come back."

"You're probably right, there," Slade replied. "We'll get this into the station, see if we can trace any prints."

"You won't find prints on that," she replied. "Not even mine. I used tongs to get it to the counter."

"Good thinking. But you never know. People slip up and that's when we nab 'em."

"This intruder managed to get this into my house with an officer out there watching and another one sleeping in my guest room."

A knock at the door caused Warrior to bark.

"Stay back but ask who it is."

Kaitlin called out, "Who's there?"

"Officer Ross" came the reply.

Slade kept his gun at the ready but opened the door to let the officer inside.

Valerie came up the steps and entered before Slade could shut the door. "Nothing," she said, shaking her head.

"I didn't find anything, either," the young man said. "But someone wanted me to look. They threw a small limb right up on the hood of my vehicle, then ran away."

"You saw someone?" Slade asked, his stomach churning.

"Just a shadow. A man wearing a black mask."

"Like a ski mask?" Slade asked.

"Yes, sir. That's what it looked like."

"He lured you away while someone went onto the porch to leave a message." He pointed to the note on the counter. Then he looked at Kaitlin. "We'd better check the entire house."

Valerie eased into the kitchen and headed toward the back porch.

"Don't you think they're long gone?" the officer asked.

Slade's gaze settled on Kaitlin. "Yep. But…they might have left behind something even worse than a threatening note."

SEVEN

"Nothing."

Valerie held her gun down and shook her head. "I can't find anything, not even a shoe print."

Slade wiped a hand down his face. It had been a long night and now dawn was creeping through the trees to the east. "We'll go over it again in the light of day." He glanced toward where Kaitlin sat staring, Warrior by her side. "Maybe she should have let Warrior have a go at things earlier."

Valerie shot a sympathetic glimpse at Kaitlin. "She didn't want anything to happen to Warrior. I think she's right. If she had let him out, they could have killed him or nabbed him and possibly her, too. They set this up to distract us, and it almost worked."

Slade had to agree. If Warrior had gone after the prowler who'd hit the cruiser with that limb, the dog might be gone forever. And Kaitlin would have gone after the animal if he hadn't returned. An easy way for her to go missing, too.

"I guess you're right. But we have to search the perimeter of her yard again and take this note in to be analyzed."

Valerie glared at the white sheet of paper that lay on the counter. "I'll make sure the crime scene techs handle it with care."

Slade didn't worry on that matter. But he was worried about the woman sitting on the couch. He walked over to Kaitlin and settled down on the storage bench in front of the bright green sofa. "How you doing?"

She shrugged, wrapped her arms across her stomach. "I just need a good night's sleep."

"You'll get one," he assured her. "I'll be your patrol tonight."

She gave him a soul-searching stare. "You don't have to do that."

"I can't keep you safe if I depend on other people. Both of these officers did their jobs and yet, you were threatened again."

"So you intend to do it yourself, right?"

He set his jaw. "I feel better doing things myself."

"You need to sleep, too."

"I don't sleep."

He didn't dare tell her that he was bone weary and dead on his feet. He'd find some shut-eye here and there. He always did.

"What do we do now?" she asked, her hand on Warrior's stubby dark gold fur. "I don't like sitting around like a target."

He blinked and then rubbed his eyes. "I'll be here tonight. Then, unless something else happens, Melody will take over. You'll be with Francine and her family this weekend."

Kaitlin shot off the couch, causing Warrior to woof out in surprise. She went to the window and paced around. "I can't be comfortable in my own home or anywhere else. Two nights in a row, this person has taunted me. At your house and, if that wasn't bold enough, now at my own home with two officers and a police dog watching over me. Who is this man?"

* * *

Slade wondered that same thing back at his office.

After briefing the entire unit on this latest development, he felt even more sure now that The Boss was not only targeting Kaitlin, but had to be after Slade, too. This was becoming way too personal. Now the culprit was leaving threatening messages. What next?

He didn't want to think about that.

But he did think about what Melody and Parker had suggested to him the day before. Picking up his phone, he scrolled through the numbers until he found Dante's cell number. Should he call his friend to say hello and see how he was doing, maybe thank him for the contribution?

It was a start. He hit the call button and waited.

"Dante Frears." His friend's smooth, confident voice echoed through the airwaves.

"Dante, it's Slade. How ya doing?"

"Good. Great. Hey, I'm glad you called. I'm having a get-together next weekend and wanted to invite you over. Bring a date if you want. It's just a casual thing by the pool."

Slade sat up in his seat. Coincidence or a carefully planned event? "What's the occasion?"

"It's Yvette's birthday. She wanted a pool party with just a few friends. Can you come by?"

"I'll certainly try," Slade replied. "And I might actually bring a date."

Dante chuckled. "Are you finally dating again?"

"No, not really." He thought about Kaitlin. "Just hanging around with a friend in need." He'd like to date her.

"Well, bring that lady friend over, man. It's been ages since we've gotten together."

"I was at that fund-raiser soiree you had last month, remember?" Slade hoped he didn't sound harsh, but Dante should at least acknowledge that he had been there since they'd talked a lot that night and Slade had thanked him several times for his contribution to the K-9 Unit.

"Oh, yeah. Of course I remember. That was a great shindig, huh?"

"The best," Slade replied. "By the way, you should see the new K-9 we're training. An all-purpose officer." He didn't mention Warrior by name. "He'll be able to sniff out anything from dead bodies to drugs to what kind of shampoo you use."

"Impressive," Dante replied, his tone not so cheery now. "I'm glad my money could help you obtain another K-9. We want to keep the streets of Sagebrush safe, don't we?"

"Of course we do," Slade said. He wanted to ask his friend if he really meant that. But he didn't. He couldn't tip his hand right now. Slade would have to play this light, stay cool and pretend nothing major was going on. "Okay, well, just called to thank you again and tell you about the new trainee. We appreciate all your support."

Dante laughed again. "Sure, man. Hope you can make it to the birthday get-together. I'll send someone by with an official invite just to remind you." Then he said, "Hey, Slade, why don't you come by soon and bring that new trainee, too. I'd love to see the dog in action."

"I might be able to swing that," Slade replied, wondering why Dante wanted to see Warrior. But then, if he was the Ski Mask Man and The Boss, he'd want to see the dog that his money had paid for—and maybe get a kick out of knowing that he was the one behind Rio's kidnapping at the same time.

Could his old friend really be that sick and twisted?

Slade thought back over the last two years since his wife had died. Dante had been the first person in the door to comfort him, bring him food and offer him anything that money could buy. Why would his best friend cause him that much heartache and pain? What had Angie ever done to Dante?

Slade thought back over the fight they'd had that day, about Angie's accusations that Slade loved his job more than he loved her and their son. She'd being angry at him for being out late at night, and being in dangerous situations.

Slade stopped, got up to wander around his office.

"You're in on drug busts. You shot a teenager a few years back, Slade. What if that kid had fired back? What if you're the one who gets the bullet next time?" Angie had said.

Why would Angie purposely remind him of that—to hurt him, to make him feel guilty all over again? Had she been talking to someone close to the situation? Or someone who was concerned about the boy being shot?

Dante?

Angie and Dante had always been close. But then, most red-blooded women were drawn to Dante's good looks and quicksilver eyes. Strange, unusual eyes. Even more silver than Slade's own blue eyes.

Eyes that were so recognizable, they'd have to be disguised in order for Dante to hide. Slade looked at the calendar. He had a few days before Dante's party. He was going to do some checking with the crime lab about black vans. Maybe they could establish some sort of connection there.

And then next week, he could also take Warrior to the house and just see the K-9's reaction. But what if the dog alerted to Dante? Slade would make some excuse. Warrior was a trainee, after all. Or better yet, he could invite Dante to the training yard. That might be the best plan since he'd mentioned showing off Warrior to Dante, anyway.

That would keep both Kaitlin and Warrior in a controlled situation that could protect them. It would also give Slade a chance to observe Dante and Warrior together.

Valerie walked into his office, tapping on the open door to alert him. Slade turned. "Yeah, what's up?"

"The crime scene team seems to think we ought to be able to track that paper back to two shops here in town."

"Really?" Since they did live in a medium-sized city, it might be possible to trace certain papers to certain stores. "But we have several office supply stores all over town."

Valerie sat down across from him. "But one of the techs says his mother-in-law buys fancy paper at a certain store in the antique district. Parchment, crisp and almond colored. He remembers it because she made such a fuss over using it for her annual Christmas letters. You know the kind where the sender goes on and on about the wonderful year they've had?"

"I know the kind," Slade said with a cynical smile. "Is this that kind of paper?"

Valerie nodded. "We don't have the high-tech means to prove it, but some good old-fashioned footwork just might."

"Good enough for now," Slade replied. "Even if we can't prove it, we might at least be able to compare this paper to that and find out who in town might keep a supply of it."

"Exactly, and who in town might have ordered that particular weight and texture recently," Valerie added. "It's just a hunch, a guessing game."

"We'll put Melody on that one if she can be spared," Slade said. "Thanks."

Valerie left smiling. Everyone would be smiling if they got a break in this case. Just a tiny break could bring about some new action.

That or...something else unthinkable might happen to someone he cared about.

* * *

Kaitlin pulled her small SUV into the driveway of her house and let Warrior out. The dog immediately headed toward the front door, his nose moving from the floor to the air.

He turned at the door, waiting for her, then ran back to her, still sniffing.

"What do you detect, Warrior?" she asked, wishing the dog could tell her his thoughts. She knew that wasn't possible, but trained K-9 dogs could communicate with body language. And Warrior's body language spoke volumes. He'd probably picked up on the scent of the intruder who'd been here last night. Could it have been someone the dog knew already, someone Warrior was so comfortable with he hadn't alerted?

That sent a chilling tickle of dread down her spine.

"It's okay," she said, looking back toward the street. A cruiser had pulled up right behind her. Slade had called her earlier and said he'd bring home dinner.

Bring home dinner.

The words had a nice ring. What would it be like to have him with her at dinner every night? To watch Caleb play with Warrior and old Chief and hopefully Rio, Mr. McNeal hovering nearby while she and Slade put together a meal? Memories of her own childhood shot like bright sparks of light inside her brain. Her mother had always made things special, probably to overcompensate for the lack of a father in the house. Then her grandmother and her aunt had done the same after she'd moved here.

It would be nice to have someone to come home to, people around who loved her and wanted to ask her about her day.

Just a dream, she told herself as she gave Warrior the hand signal to search and stood back before she entered the house. When Warrior returned, looking both disappointed and hopeful, she figured her house was safe for now.

She went in and found Warrior's favorite toy and rewarded him with some toss and fetch. After Warrior had tired of the game, she sorted through the mail she'd taken out of the box beside the front door. A water bill, a bank statement, two catalogues, but nothing ominous. No one had left her any cryptic notes today. But the day was still young.

A shiver ran down her spine. Kaitlin had never been afraid in her own house but now, even with Warrior prowling around, she couldn't help but feel the claws of apprehension ripping at her skin. She didn't like being so vulnerable, so exposed. She didn't like being a target for someone's greed and revenge. The person behind that black mask was a cruel, misguided soul, an evil person.

She closed her eyes and asked God to protect her and those she loved, a verse from Thessalonians popping in her mind: *But the Lord is faithful, and He will strengthen you and protect you from the evil one.*

Where had she heard that? Oh, at her mother's funeral, of course. The verse had made her angry back then but now it made her stop and think. And it calmed her jittery nerves.

Thinking back over last night, she remembered Slade telling her he was going to have dinner with her tonight. *That* was both a comfort and a distraction. She could handle having a girlfriend helping her to stay safe, but Slade McNeal in the flesh? Dinner with the captain. She'd probably forget all about the pizza.

What would they do? Sit there staring at each other until Valerie got here?

Okay, you'll also have Officer Ross out in the cruiser.

He'll be on alert and he works the night shift so he doesn't fall asleep on the job—ever.

She should be glad she had so many protectors, but she also wanted her life back to normal. If this went on much longer…

A car pulling into the driveway curtailed her thoughts. Slade was here and she hadn't even freshened up yet. Quickly running a hand down her ponytail, she grabbed her purse and slapped on some lip gloss then found a mint to pop into her mouth.

Silly measures since she had no intention of flirting with the man who'd vowed to save her. She didn't need saving. She just needed this stalker off the streets. She intended to work with the K-9 unit and the entire police department to make that happen. And she intended to keep training Warrior with every ounce of energy she had, so the dog would be ready for duty soon enough. That's really all she wanted or needed.

But when she looked out the window and saw Slade carrying a pizza box, his dark uniform making him look official and formidable, she wondered what else she needed.

A good man would sure be nice.

Especially a good man who'd brought home her favorite pizza.

EIGHT

"I wish you could have brought Caleb with you."

Slade glanced up at Kaitlin, the longing of her comment hitting him in the gut. "Me, too. But he's safe with Papa and Nanny Blanche. Not to mention the night nurse, Jasper. That man could split an oak with his bare hands."

She leaned across the table, her slice of pizza half-eaten. "But Caleb could be in danger, too. I'm not judging you for bringing me dinner. Just suggesting that I'm an adult and I can take care of myself. He can't."

"And he's surrounded by people who are aware of the situation," Slade retorted. "Do you think I'd leave him if I didn't believe that?"

"I know you," she replied. "I trust your judgment. But I can't help but worry, Slade. I'd never get over it if something happened to him while you're here with me."

Slade got up to get some more iced tea. "Are you trying to drive me nuts? I've thought of everything you just mentioned but I do this job every day. I've hired people trained to help my son and my father and I check on them all the time."

"I didn't mean to imply you don't care," she said, her eyes downcast. "I'm sorry."

Slade sat back down and stared at the pizza, his appetite

gone for now. "Sorry I got so defensive, but that's a sore subject with me. I enjoy my job but the long hours and the midnight calls, plus me being a single dad takes its toll. I get a little hot under the collar when people ask me how I can leave my boy." He tapped his fingers on the wooden table, wondering if he hadn't jumped at an excuse to be with her tonight. Wondering and knowing he felt personally responsible for her attack the other day. "Let's just say it's not an easy decision and leave it at that."

"Good idea." She finished her meal, then sat staring out into the growing dusk. "I think I'm a little embarrassed, having all this security. I worked the beat for a little over a year, but then when the chance to become a trainer came up, I jumped at it. I sometimes wonder if I made the right decision."

"You don't like your job?"

"No, I mean, yes. I love my job. But did I change course because I wanted to work with animals…or did I do it because deep down inside, I'm a coward?"

"Did you like being a patrol officer?"

She glanced out the window. "I didn't hate it. But I always felt like there was something else for me. My instincts told me I'd be better suited to the K-9 division, working as a trainer."

"And you're good at that job."

She smiled at the compliment. "I do enjoy the work, but it also puts a filter between me and the hard stuff."

"Training an animal from the time he's a puppy till the time he makes his first find is nothing to sneeze at, Kaitlin. I think you're right where you're supposed to be."

"Me, too," she said, relief coloring her cute freckles. "That's why it's so odd, being someone's target."

"Yep. Odd and a pain for all of us. But we're gonna crack this case." He told her about what Valerie and the crime techs had decided regarding the paper. "If we can get a match, any match, we can narrow down how many people have purchased that particular paper recently. It's a long shot, but it's something."

"Amazing," she said. "And a good call. Valerie has moved from rookie to a good officer."

"Well, she does have a Rottweiler for a partner. And Lexi is a good, solid apprehension dog that you helped to train. Maybe we should have let her bring Lexi last night. She could bring her when she comes over later."

Kaitlin shrugged. "And let another officer dog get kidnapped or worse? I don't think so. I worry about Warrior getting caught in the cross-fire."

"I don't think they'll harm the animals unless they get frustrated and give up. They need them alive."

"And then, they'd just…get rid of the animals?"

"Or let them go. I hope every day that Rio will show up at my door."

She glanced over at where Warrior lay snoozing in his soft, square doggie bed. "I hope and pray for that, too. I won't give up."

Slade saw the determination in her eyes. She had something to prove, but he hoped she didn't try to use this episode to show the world she was capable of facing down the enemy on her own. "You stick with what you know best. Train Warrior and let the rest work itself out."

"I'll give you and the team one week, Slade," she replied. Getting up to clear away the empty pizza box, she pivoted at the counter. "After that, no more patrols or protection. I want my life back. I know the protocol, I know the rules. I know what to watch for now. And I mean what I say—you can't camp out here the rest of your life."

Slade let the thought of spending the rest of his life around her settle over him before he brushed it away. That would be nice, but that was just a silly dream. This was reality, and he had no doubt that this woman would bolt in exactly one week. She seemed determined to show the world she was more than capable of doing things her way. Why was she so stubborn about accepting help?

"You sure drive a hard bargain. I don't like working with a ticking clock over my head."

"The clock was already ticking," she retorted. "And time is running out."

"You don't pull any punches, do you?"

She shook her head. "I don't have time to be wishy-washy."

Slade understood that concept. "Neither do I. But I can't promise you I'll have this all wrapped up within a week."

"I didn't say that," she replied, already heading toward the hallway, Warrior right behind her. "I said I won't need any protection after a week." She turned at the arched opening between the kitchen and den and the hallway. "After that, I'll take matters into my own hands. I haven't forgotten how to use a weapon."

"Kaitlin?"

She waved off what she must have known would be a warning. "I'm going to take a shower."

Slade didn't call after her. But he didn't intend to let her take anything into her own hands. She was brave. Too brave. That could be a good trait or that could get her killed.

He wouldn't let that happen.

His cell buzzed. "McNeal."

"Sir, it's Valerie Salgado. I heard back about the stationery."

"And?"

"I recognized one of the names on the list of people who'd purchased that type of paper in the last month or so."

"What name?"

"Yvette Frears. I believe she's the wife of your friend Dante?"

"Yes. Correct." Slade rubbed his temple. "Thank you, Officer Salgado. Let's keep this quiet for now. I need to see the other names on the list before I do some investigating."

"I understand."

Slade ended the call and sat staring out into the dusk. Could be coincidence. Could be a big break in this case. Had Dante taken a piece of his wife's stationery? Or had Yvette herself left that note? But why would she?

He got up, then thought about the birthday party at Dante's place this weekend. Kaitlin had no idea Dante might be behind all of this and right now, Slade wanted to keep things that way. But he wanted to keep an eye on her, too. Would he put her in even more danger by taking her inside Dante's house?

Or would it be the perfect chance to see his friend's reaction to Kaitlin Mathers?

Kaitlin emerged about thirty minutes later, freshly showered and wearing her old cut-off jean shorts and a scoop-necked T-shirt with her old broken-in pink flip-flops.

She found Slade pacing in front of the slightly drawn blinds in the den, talking on his phone.

"Well, that's good that Nanny Blanche made you cupcakes. No, I won't be home to read to you tonight. Papa can read a little bit maybe. Or maybe Jasper will help Papa read, okay?" He turned when he heard Warrior's paws tapping against the wooden floors. "All right. Be good for Nanny Blanche, okay? I'll come by and see you before preschool in the morning."

Kaitlin smiled when he hung up. "How's Caleb?"

"He seems in a fairly good mood today. I never know. If he has a bad dream, it tends to ruin his whole day."

"And yours?" She shot him a sympathetic look. "I'm sorry I pushed you earlier. I know you're a good dad."

He gave her a skeptical glance. "I try, but I'm not sure it's ever enough." He put his phone away. "I know how it looks to some people, though, but I've got to work for a living."

Not sure if that comment was directed at her, Kaitlin began cleaning up the den. "I'm not usually this messy. Last night was tough so I didn't tidy up this morning."

"My house is much worse than this," he said, his gaze moving all around her. "I can't remember the last time I saw you out of your training uniform."

Kaitlin remembered, but she wouldn't tell him that. He'd dropped Caleb by on a rare Saturday, apologizing because his dad was sick and the babysitter was out of town. Kaitlin had been happy to help out, and she and Caleb had spent part of the day in the park and the other part at a kiddie restaurant. Slade had found them in the backyard, playing catch. She'd been tired, sweaty and without makeup. That hadn't mattered too much back then, and it burned her that it was beginning to matter now.

So she decided to be practical. "I was worn out from the heat. That shower helped." She pushed at her wet hair. "You're welcome to use the bathroom."

"I showered at the gym," he said. "I brought a change of clothes just in case." He pointed to a duffel bag by the door. "I try to prepare for anything."

"Okay."

The room went silent. Then she smiled to herself. He'd talked to her more during dinner than in all the times they'd been around each other in the past. Maybe the captain was warming up to her. Or maybe he was just doing his job.

He cleared his throat. "Kaitlin, you didn't mean what you said earlier, did you?"

"About taking matters into my own hands?"

"That would be it, yes."

"I need to brush up on my target practice," she said with a matter-of-fact shrug.

"So you were serious."

"I have to be, Slade. I won't live in fear. It took me too long to get over what happened to my mother."

She sank down in her favorite chair and motioned for him to join her. "Do you want something to drink?"

"I'm good." He settled on the couch, facing the door. "And I'm sorry about your mom. But you don't have to be a hero."

"I'm no hero," she retorted, tired of this conversation. "But I'll do what I have to do to protect myself. Or anyone else those thugs try to hurt."

His brow furrowed in worry. "Let us handle this."

"I will, for now."

He stared at her, let out a sigh, then shook his head. "Okay. Enough for now." Then he leaned forward. "I have a better idea."

Her heart pumped a warning at the questioning look in his eyes. What did the man have in mind?

"Uh, I've been invited to a birthday party at my friend Dante Frears's house this weekend. I thought you might like to attend with me."

Shocked, Kaitlin didn't know what to say. "So you can keep an eye on me, Captain? Or as your date?"

He grinned, then rubbed a hand down his five o'clock shadow. "Well, I guess a little of both."

A bold step for him, she decided. "Killing two birds with one stone?"

He looked confused, then his expression changed to reserved, almost cautious. "I'd like you to go with me, yes. But I'd also like to keep my eye on you, even when you're there with me."

Kaitlin picked up on the intensity of his eyes. "Why is this so important?"

He shifted on the couch, but never took his eyes off her. "Because I can't be in two places at once. I promised Dante I'd be at his wife's birthday party and...I want to keep you safe, too."

She had to mess with him a little bit. "That does create a dilemma, doesn't it?"

Another shift, then he settled back, one leg bent over the other knee. "You're trying to make this way harder than it needs to be."

"Am I? It just seems out of character for you to be going to a party in the middle of this investigation, and it also seems strange that you'd want me to go along."

He leaned forward again. "I have my reasons, so I'd appreciate it if you'd cut me some slack and just say you'll go with me."

Kaitlin wondered what was behind this sudden need to have her with him at this particular party. Did he know something he wasn't telling her? Did she want to know?

Deciding she'd be wise to keep her eye on him, too, she finally nodded. "Sounds good to me. I can't turn down a party at the Frears penthouse. It's all swag and swank."

"It is that." He breathed what looked like a big sigh of relief. "It should be interesting. And fun."

"Fun? Do you actually ever have fun, Captain?"

He grinned at that. "I've been known to let my hair down, thank you very much."

She didn't see how his crisp, short hair could ever be let down, but it would be nice to see him in a relaxed atmosphere away from work and all the tension of this case.

"It'll be worth the trouble to see you out of uniform."

"Really?"

She put a hand to her mouth, realizing that hadn't come out the way she meant. "You know what I mean. I meant—you're always working." She stopped, laughed. "I'll stop digging that hole and agree to go."

"Good. Dante has the means to throw lavish parties, so it should be not only fun but interesting."

"Yes, it should be. I'll look forward to going with you."

But she had to wonder—if this was supposed to be such an enjoyable event, why wasn't the man smiling?

NINE

Kaitlin waved to Valerie as they parted ways the next morning in the parking lot. “Thanks again. I appreciate you spending the night. It was nice of your neighbor to stay with Bethany.”

“No problem,” Valerie replied, smiling at the mention of the toddler niece she was raising. “I enjoyed all our girl talk last night. We covered everything regarding my wedding plans.”

“Me, too.” Kaitlin yawned. “I think we stayed up too late.”

Valerie nodded. “But…at least we didn’t have any prowlers or notes underneath the door.”

“Thanks again,” Kaitlin said, lowering her voice since other workers were showing up.

Valerie gave her a big smile, then headed for the K-9 Unit’s offices. Kaitlin went to her own cubbyhole of an office and got ready to start her day. Grabbing her equipment, play toys and water bottle, she headed out with an eager Warrior.

Slade was waiting for her in the yard. “So you had an uneventful night.”

“We watched sappy movies and talked about weddings.”

He lowered his gaze, clearly uncomfortable with that

conversation. "Uh…that's good. No noises, no intruders, notes?"

Touched by his concern, she smiled at him. "Slade, we were fine. I told you everything would be okay, and it was. I don't think the intruder will be back now that the heat's on."

"Good. I intend to keep it that way, too." He turned to leave, then stopped to pet Warrior. "I'll see you later."

Kaitlin kept her smile intact, but inside she wondered how long any of them could keep this up. For most of this year, people on the team or involved with team members had been under siege. Slade couldn't keep carrying this burden much longer.

"Help us, Lord," she whispered as she grabbed some gear and started Warrior through his warm-up. "Help all of us to fight this attack."

She glanced up and looked around the yard. Just a normal summer day. The sun drew a path over the crusty, worn grass, promising more heat to come. A sneaky wind moved in and out of the big oaks, causing shadows to dapple and dance across the asphalt behind the yard. Cars revved to life, traffic honked and braked. A normal workday, except that each time Kaitlin glanced toward the back parking lot gate, she thought about being held at gunpoint by a man with blacked-out eyes.

In spite of the warm morning sun, a shiver wormed its way down her spine and a cold chill centered inside her heart.

Slade stared out into the bright sunshine, remembering how a few days ago he'd watched a masked man hold a gun to Kaitlin's head. Watched, fired and let the man get away.

He wouldn't miss next time. And his gut told him there would be a next time.

His phone rang. Dante.

"Captain McNeal," Slade answered.

"So formal. You must be in your office."

"You know me well," Slade replied, his gut burning again. "What's up?"

"Just checking to make sure you can make it this weekend. Yvette is excited that you're bringing a date."

Slade managed a passable chuckle. "Just a friend, nothing to get too excited about." He wouldn't tell Dante anything that might fuel the attack on Kaitlin. Reminding himself his buddy was innocent until proven guilty, he cleared his throat. "I talked to my friend last night. We'll be there."

"Good. Glad to hear it. I've been so busy this summer, it'll be nice to kick back and relax. How are things going on your end? You're still searching for Rio, right?"

An innocent question, or was Dante fishing for information? Slade decided to be careful with every word that came out of his mouth. "We're still on the case. We've eliminated some suspects, but we have our eye on others. That's about all I can say at this point."

"Vague as always," Dante retorted. Did Slade imagine the hint of sarcasm in that statement? "It goes with the job, as you always tell me."

"I'm afraid so," Slade replied. "That's the nature of my line of work."

"And you're good at your job." Dante chuckled into the phone. "It sure will be great to catch up and reminisce about the old days."

"Yeah, great. We'll see you Saturday night."

"Looking forward to it."

Slade hung up, his mind reeling with suspicion and anger. Last night, he'd done what he usually did every night when the house was quiet. He'd gone back over this case with an eagle eye, but this time he'd tried to place Dante in the middle of things. As much as he hated to see it, some things were beginning to add up.

Dante had the means to run a huge crime operation. With his money, he had the ability to hire people who'd be more than willing to keep silent and do the dirty work. And with his intimidating, commanding presence, he'd surely take care of anyone who crossed him. Someone within the organization had double-crossed The Boss, since the mysterious criminal had purposely taken out several of his own people. Dante had never liked being tricked or betrayed. Slade had seen him angry on more than one occasion for some small slight. Slade had even been on the receiving end of Dante's anger before, but they'd always worked things out.

But where was the motive? Dante was a smart man, a self-made man who'd come home after their Middle-Eastern tour of duty to become a real-estate mogul. That had led to other business venues and a lot of opportunities to make some serious money. Had he become so greedy that he'd forgotten what he'd been fighting for over there and decided to turn to the dark side?

The opportunities for such a career were certainly staring all of them in the face. West Texas was known for being a corridor for illegal activities. Slade had been fighting those activities since the day he'd become a police officer.

He and Dante had served together, fought together and come home together. At times, they'd gone their separate ways and drifted apart. *But we always found our way back,* Slade thought.

Dante had never forsaken the camaraderie they'd built serving their country. And neither had Slade.

But what if his friend had forsaken his honor for greed? And what if Melody and Parker were right about Daniel being Dante's son? Slade had put a bullet in Daniel's leg, but someone else had killed the boy. Jim Wheaton, a cop gone bad. A cop who was now dead. Did Dante know Jim had made that shot?

When Slade looked at all the details of this case and placed Dante as The Boss, things began to make more sense. But he hated the idea that a man who'd been his friend for most of their adult lives might be behind all of these criminal activities. A man who could possibly be charged with multiple murders.

Could that man be Dante Frears?

What if Slade had to take down the comrade who'd saved his life on the battlefield?

Kaitlin heard the doorbell, her heart jumping ahead of her. Slade. Right on time.

"You look great," Francine told her, one finger putting the finishing touches on Kaitlin's upswept hair. "Now relax and have fun."

Kaitlin took one last look in her bedroom mirror. Her friend had helped her put her hair up in a loose chignon. It was elegant but not too fussy. She'd put on extra mascara and a deeper pink lipstick and a sweep of shadow and blush.

"I don't look overdone, do I?"

Francine shook her head. "You look good. So good that Captain McNeal is gonna pop an eyeball looking."

"I don't want that to happen," Kaitlin said as she grabbed her tiny white clutch purse and glanced at her dress one more time. "The dress?"

"Is to die for," Francine retorted, her gaze moving down the floral chiffon. "It looks summery but casual. Why you don't wear this thing more is beyond me."

"I've never had anywhere to wear it," Kaitlin reminded

her. She'd bought it on a whim after finding it on a clearance rack at the local department store. "It does feel great against my legs."

"And you look great wearing it." Francine pushed her toward the front door. "Now go before the man breaks the door down."

"Thanks for helping me," Kaitlin said, her hand on Warrior's head. "So...I'll see you two back at your house after the party."

"Yes, ma'am." Francine winked, then stepped back. "Have fun, okay?"

Kaitlin opened the door and found Slade standing there wearing black slacks and a stark sky-blue polo shirt that brought out the deep blue of his eyes.

"Hi," she said, her suddenly dry throat making her tone gravelly.

Slade's gaze slid down her dress. "Hi. Wow. I mean, you look great."

Francine clapped her hands, causing Slade's gaze to shift to Kaitlin's. "Hello, Francine."

"Hi, Captain. She does look great, and I helped."

He laughed at Francine's antics. "You did a good job."

Kaitlin basked in his warm gaze. This was beginning to feel like a real date. That should make her nervous, but she felt elated and...safe. Slade made her feel safe. Not very romantic, but so vital on her list.

"Are you ready?" he asked, his smile tentative.

"I am." She turned back to Warrior and patted his head again. "Be good for Franny, okay, boy?"

Warrior barked and pranced, clearly confused at seeing his mistress in a dress. His dark brown eyes held a quizzical kind of adoration that made Kaitlin's heart melt.

"Go," Francine said, pushing her toward Slade.

Slade took her arm in his and chuckled after Francine shut the door. "She's a good friend."

"Yes. A little pushy, but the best."

"She's also a good trainer."

"Warrior sure thinks so. She's going to give him some play time at her house. I hope you don't mind dropping me off there after the party."

"No. I want to make sure you do go there. You can't be home alone yet."

"Yes, Captain," she said in a cheeky tone.

"Don't let that ruin our night," he replied.

Kaitlin wondered again why this night was so important to him. "Are you going to relax and enjoy this party?"

"I hope so. I'll try."

She hadn't missed the tension in him. Something was up with him, but then he was always edgy, even on a good day. She'd have to watch out for him tonight. Slade McNeal was known for putting others first. Maybe it was time someone put him first.

But when he pulled his father's sedan up to the apartment complex where Dante Frears lived, she let out a giggle. "Wow, this building *is* so fancy."

"You seem surprised. You do know that Dante is a successful businessman."

"Everyone knows that and everyone knows about his penthouse. Of course, I rarely get this far downtown twice in a row."

Slade hit the steering wheel. "You were at the big fundraiser last month at the Sagebrush Hotel."

"Nice of you to remember."

Slade found a spot in the parking garage. "I think the whole department was at that affair. But tonight, he promised just a few friends." He parked the vehicle and came around to help her out. "Did you speak to him that night?"

"Uh, no. The place was packed and Melody wasn't feeling good. We left early."

"Should be more relaxed tonight."

The undercurrent of tension filled the air. "You don't seem comfortable about this."

Slade put his hand on her back. "I'm *not* comfortable about this."

So he'd admitted that much, at least. Kaitlin knew not to push him. But his stoic words only reinforced her need to protect him in the same way he wanted to protect her. She didn't know why she suddenly felt this way. But her instincts told her that Slade being friends with such a powerful, pretentious man didn't ring true.

Did she dare ask him about that friendship?

She didn't get a chance. Some other people came up and Slade started talking to them and then introduced her. They all rode the elevator up to the penthouse, the scent of expensive perfume and aftershave tickling Kaitlin's nostrils.

When the doors opened, Kaitlin had to gather her thoughts. So much glitter and glamour, so many of Sagebrush society's movers and shakers. She felt as out of place as a catfish at a lobster fest.

Dante and his wife, Yvette, were out by the rooftop pool, but the couple immediately came inside the thrown-open sliding doors that made up one wall to greet them.

"Slade!" Dante flashed his white teeth right along with his gold and diamond signet ring. "Man, it's so good to see you again."

"Same here," Slade said, his tone not quite so chipper and artificial. "Dante, this is Kaitlin Mathers. She's one of our top K-9 trainers."

Dante took Kaitlin's hand in his, his silver-blue eyes gleaming with interest. "So nice to see the woman who got Slade McNeal out of the house on a Saturday night. But I think we've met before, maybe."

"Possibly a few weeks ago when we all attended the fund-raiser gala." Kaitlin smiled and pulled her hand away. "It's nice to once again see the benefactor of such a generous donation. We really appreciate it, Mr. Frears. I'm sure Slade has mentioned I'm already training a very special dog, partly because of your funding."

Dante's beautiful dark-haired wife stepped forward, her arm possessively on her husband, her dangling golden earrings sparkling. "We totally support the K-9 Unit here in Sagebrush. Dante and I were honored to make the donation." She glanced at Slade. "I hope you find Rio soon, Slade. Dante keeps me up-to-date on the generalities."

"We're always on the case," Slade said, his tone firm but polite.

Kaitlin didn't miss the tension radiating off his body, though. She glanced around at the opulent room filled with gold-colored accessories and white leather. The penthouse was elegant and overdone, but that was just her opinion. The pool glistened in the late-day sun, floating candles taking over where the breathtaking sunset left off.

Kaitlin brought her gaze back to the moment and found Dante Frears staring at her with icy silver eyes that reminded her of a wolf. A shiver hit her neckline and worked down her arms.

Slade must have sensed her discomfort. He took her arm and smiled at his friend. "I think I'll show Kaitlin the pool and that view you paid too much money for."

"Enjoy it," Dante said, holding out his hand to entice them. "Yvette will have someone bring you two a drink." He moved on to the next guests coming in the door.

Yvette's smile seemed as forced as Dante's brittle laugh. "What can I get you?"

Slade asked for a soda and Kaitlin ordered water with lemon.

"Not heavy drinkers, I see," Yvette said with a soft smile. "I'll send your refreshments right over."

Kaitlin glanced over at Slade after Yvette left, but he'd turned his head toward where Dante stood with two other men. Kaitlin didn't miss the hint of a frown on Slade's face.

She didn't fit into this kind of world, but she held her head high for the captain's sake. Maybe later, he would open up about his relationship with Dante Frears.

Until then, she'd do whatever Slade needed her to do while they were here. Because in her heart, she knew this visit was about a lot more than a birthday party.

TEN

As the evening wore on, Slade tried to memorize things that would give him clues to Dante's character. He noticed Frears never set his plate and utensils down anywhere. Yvette or one of the waiters was always there to take his dishes and wineglasses away. Odd, but then, Dante demanded efficiency, and he had some strange quirks regarding neatness and cleanliness. Slade did remember that about his old friend. Even in the middle of the desert, he had demanded neatness and order as often as possible.

Throughout the night, Yvette seemed relaxed and moved through the crowd with an easy elegance. But every now and then, Slade would catch her staring at her husband, a hint of worry in her eyes. Deciding to visit with her in hopes of hearing something that might give him a clue, Slade made his way to where she stood out by the pool. When she saw him coming, she smiled and disengaged herself from the group of women she'd been conversing with. Slade nodded at her, then turned to make sure Kaitlin was safe. She stood with another group who'd heard she was a K-9 trainer. They were asking her questions about the program. Right now, Kaitlin seemed to glow with pride while she discussed the subject near and dear to her heart.

Which made her even more near and dear to Slade.

"Are you having a good time?" Yvette asked, her arm on Slade's shoulder, her gaze following his.

"Yes. The food's great and it's good to see some friends."

"You don't come by enough these days," she replied, again sweeping the area behind Slade with a sharp eye.

Was she looking for her husband?

"I apologize for that," Slade said. "But I did tell Dante I wanted him to see the newest K-9 officer dog we've been training. The funds y'all donated helped to make that possible. Kaitlin is doing a great job on that."

Yvette's dark eyes seemed to brighten. "She's really lovely, Slade. Very girl-next-door. Seems perfect for you."

Slade didn't miss the hint of censure in that comment. Yvette had never liked Angie. The two used to spar and throw out catty remarks at each other. Pushing that particular memory away, he said, "Kaitlin is a good person. We're really just friends. But…we are both single. Who knows."

Yvette grinned at that. "I think I see a spark of interest in those blue eyes of yours."

He only laughed, but he couldn't deny it. He was interested in Kaitlin. Right now, however, he was interested in keeping her safe. Maybe when this case was solved—

Yvette waved to someone across the room. "Excuse me, Slade. I need to talk to Rachel about our meeting next week."

"Of course." Slade watched her go, then decided this might be a good time to go find a bathroom. If he ever wanted to get a sample of Dante's DNA, now was the time.

Kaitlin glanced around, looking for Slade. When she saw him heading toward the back of the house she figured he was searching for a bathroom. But when he glanced around, she noticed the covert expression she'd seen on the faces of many cops. Was Slade on the case? She'd wait for him beside the big, empty fireplace near the hallway door, guarding, just in case.

Making her way over there, Kaitlin looked up to see Dante staring down the hallway. Was he worried about Slade? Deciding to distract him in spite of being nervous around all of these people, Kaitlin waved a hand in his face. "Hi, Mr. Frears."

Dante tugged his gaze away from the hall and drew a smiling mask down over his frown. "Hello, there. Call me Dante, okay?"

"Okay." Kaitlin pushed at a curl dangling in her eye. "I wanted to thank you once again for helping us out. Our whole unit really wants to find Rio and get our operation back on track."

Dante's gaze turned to crystal but it melted away before Kaitlin could get rid of the goose bumps on her bare arms. "It was my pleasure. I'd do anything for Slade." He did a scan of the entire room. "Speaking of Slade, where did my buddy get off to, anyway?"

Kaitlin's heart did a warning beat. Whatever Slade was up to, she didn't think Dante needed to know about it. "I think he went to the bathroom. I'll watch for him."

Dante gave her a twisted smile. "You two seem chummy."

Kaitlin laughed, hoping it would hide the way this man made her feel. This creepy factor was odd and overwhelming, but she couldn't deny that something about Dante Frears made her feel edgy…and apprehensive. "We've been friends for a while now. He's a good man."

"Yes, of course he is." Dante gave her that cold stare again. "He loved his wife, you know. But…it wasn't enough. Men like Slade McNeal love their work more than they love the people around them. You might want to remember that, sweetheart."

Something familiar and frightening gnawed at Kaitlin's consciousness. "I'm not sure what you mean, but thank you for the advice."

"Yeah, you do know what I mean." Dante gave her another smile. "You're a big girl. You'll soon figure it out. Just consider yourself warned."

The look in his eyes seemed to say so much more. What kind of warning did he want her to hear? One about Slade? Or one about...him?

"Excuse me," he said, already moving toward the long, wide hallway. "I'm going to find Slade."

Kaitlin didn't know what to do or say, but a woman approached Dante and engaged him in conversation long enough for Kaitlin to leave her spot by the hallway and hurry outside. She'd seen another door out on the rooftop terrace. And she prayed that door would lead her to Slade so she could warn him that Dante was looking for him.

Slade slid into the shadows and worked his way toward the master bedroom on the far end of the big penthouse. He had a small paper envelope ready to take samples of Dante's hair. Hating the underhanded way he had to go about this, he rationalized that this was for his own purposes since this wouldn't hold up in court without a search warrant, anyway.

"Desperate men do desperate things."

Slade could hear his father's words of caution echoing inside his brain. How many times had Papa said that when trying to find a criminal? Slade believed it himself. Papa had been talking about criminals, but now Slade had to wonder.

Had he become desperate?

Maybe enough to risk this, at least.

He hurried across the plush, white shag carpet of the immaculate bedroom and treaded into the sprawling marble and chrome bath. After looking through a few drawers, he found a man's hairbrush and quickly donned a glove he'd tucked into his pocket so he could gather a few clumps. After he'd put the hair fibers into the small envelope and returned it and the glove to his pants pocket, he turned to leave and heard a door opening from the hallway.

Looking around, Slade realized he was trapped. A glass door at the end of the bathroom might lead to the terrace but he didn't have time to get to it. He glanced at the shower. Glass. Did he dare hide in the big closet?

To his surprise, even as he wondered who'd entered the bedroom, he also heard the door to the outside creaking open.

Whirling around, Slade awaited his fate.

And saw Kaitlin rushing toward him.

Before he could speak, she grabbed him to her and planted a long, soft kiss on his lips. "Hold me," she whispered, her lips pressing against his again.

Shocked and still full of adrenaline, Slade sank into the kiss by taking her into his arms. Kaitlin held him tight, her lips clinging to his while a soft sigh sounded in her throat. A voice in Slade's head kept telling him to stop this, but his mind seemed to spin out of control.

He liked kissing Kaitlin.

So much so, that he didn't stop until she pulled away and gasped in shock.

Slade turned to find Dante standing there, grinning at them.

"So this is where you two got off to."

"Uh, yes," Slade replied, his gaze sweeping toward Kaitlin.

The warning look in her eyes told him that she'd just saved his bacon, big time. And made him even more aware of his growing attraction to her.

"It's my fault," Kaitlin said on a breathless giggle. "I told Slade I'd find him, so I kept opening doors until I did. Hope you don't mind, Dante. You know how it is when two people first discover each other."

She glanced back at Slade, her eyes going deep with meaning and what looked like true longing.

Slade shrugged and tugged her close. "Guess we're busted. Sorry, Dante. I don't usually plan clandestine meetings like this, but we rarely get a chance to see each other away from work."

Dante kept grinning. "I have to admit this is way out of character for you, my old friend. But…can't say that I blame you one bit."

His gaze moved over Kaitlin in a way that made Slade want to punch him out. But before that could happen, Dante waved a hand in the air. "Please, don't let me stop you. Carry on. Have fun."

"We're done," Kaitlin said, looking embarrassed. "I think it's time for us to head home, anyway."

Dante took her words in the wrong way, but Slade figured it worked to their advantage. Shaking his head, Dante laughed again. "Well, at least tell the birthday girl goodnight. She's so glad you both came. And she loves the scarf you gave her, Slade."

Slade breathed a sigh of relief. "Kaitlin picked that out."

Dante gave her another probing appraisal. "You're a keeper, for sure." Then his crystallized gaze hit Slade. "You'd better take care of her, my friend."

Slade didn't miss the implications of that suggestion. Suggestion? More like a direct warning.

After Dante left, he turned to Kaitlin, his breathing

ragged with relief and concern. "We just made a fatal mistake."

Kaitlin looked confused and hurt. "I had to do something to warn you. I'm sorry." She looked away. "I shouldn't have kissed you, but I couldn't think of anything else that would convince him."

Slade drew her close. "I didn't mind the kiss, Kaitlin. But…now Dante *knows* you're important to me."

"And that's a problem because?"

He put his lips to her ear. "Because he's just become the number one suspect in this case."

Kaitlin stared out the car window until Slade pulled off the road and parked underneath a streetlight.

"We need to talk," he said, shutting off the engine.

"I think so," she retorted, still in shock from what he'd told her earlier. No wonder he'd seemed so tense. Maybe Dante was right. Maybe Slade really did put his work ahead of everything and everyone.

They were at a park near the police station. "Want to take a stroll?" he asked.

She looked around but didn't see anyone else in the beams of the security lights. "Sure."

He got out and came around to open her door. When she slid out of the car, he shut the door and held her there. "Kaitlin, what you did back there—"

"Was a huge mistake. I know."

"No, no. Listen to me." He pushed a hand down his face, his expression full of frustration.

"I make you mad," she said before he could berate her for being so foolish. "I was so worried that Dante would find you snooping, I didn't think straight. I didn't want—"

He stopped her words with a kiss of his own. A kiss that deepened and changed and caused her to sigh again.

Somewhere in all the delightful joy of kissing him, Kaitlin realized that he'd been the one to do the deed this time.

Slade was kissing her out in the open, out in the park.

But…he still had something to say.

She pulled away. "Well. I…I don't know what to say to that."

"You don't need to say anything," he replied huskily, his finger grazing her thoroughly kissed lips. "I owe you a big thanks for saving me back there." Then he touched his forehead to hers. "And in such a very good way, too."

Surprised, Kaitlin let out a breath. "So you're not mad?"

"No, but I am concerned."

"Tell me what's going on."

He motioned to a bench. Once they were settled, he stared off toward the playground. "I think Dante might be The Boss."

Kaitlin's shocked gasp echoed out over the quiet park. But now the shadows and shapes seemed to loom closer and look darker. She thought about her talk with Dante earlier, shivers etching a path across her body.

"What makes you think that?"

Slade took her hand in his. "I can't give you all the details but…I *was* snooping tonight. I was collecting DNA."

"Dante's?"

"Yes. We think he might be Daniel Jones's father."

Kaitlin thought about that. "So you need the DNA to prove that?"

"Yes, but that's only for Melody's benefit. She needs to know the truth. Even if it's a match, I obtained it illegally. I'm not proud of that, but it will at least ease my mind. Besides, there's a lot more to this case."

"DNA doesn't make your friend a criminal," she reminded him. "I mean, if you're just trying to prove he fathered Daniel, I understand. But you said there's more."

"Yep. Dante has the means and the opportunity to run a criminal operation." He held her hand tight. "I always wondered how he'd made it big so quickly after we both came back here. It didn't make sense, but I got busy with my own job and kind of ignored it. I have to admit it's always bothered me." He went silent and still for a while, then said, "My wife, Angie, used to throw that in my face. She resented Dante's wealth, but she enjoyed dropping his name, too. She thought I should go to work for him."

Kaitlin turned to stare at him. "But your heart is in police work."

He looked up at Kaitlin, an appreciative curve in his smile. "You always did get that about me."

She rested her head on his shoulder. "Of course I do. I feel the same way." She thought about Dante's warning, but put that out of her mind for now. Then she nudged Slade to continue. "What else can you tell me about Dante?"

He lifted an arm across her shoulder to tug her close. "He could have possibly killed several people involved with this."

Kaitlin's heart did that warning stampede again and the food she'd eaten at the party seemed to harden in her stomach. "What else, Slade?"

He turned and stared into her eyes. "He might also be the Ski Mask Man."

ELEVEN

Kaitlin got up off the bench and twisted around, her mind in turmoil as she relived that day. "That's it," she said, putting a hand to her mouth. "That man, his voice—"

Slade stood to steady her. "What? Did you remember something?"

She bobbed her head. "Yes. That man called me 'sweetheart.' I didn't even remember it until just now, but today while you were in the back of the house, Dante called me that, too." She shivered, held her arms together. "When he said it, I felt something, a trickle of awareness, but I couldn't make the connection."

Slade grasped her arms, pulled her close. "He's taunting both of us."

She stepped back, nodding again. "He tried to warn me about you. He said men like you love their jobs more than they do people."

Slade brought her back into his arms. "I can't argue with that. At times, I've thought that same thing. But…I don't understand why he'd resent me for doing my job. Unless, of course, he's a criminal."

Kaitlin nodded again. "And…if he is Daniel's father and he blames you for his son's death, coupled with his need for control and respect, then that makes him desperate and dangerous."

Slade let out a short breath. "He came after Rio for a reason. He needs a trained canine to help him find something in those woods."

"Do you think he murdered someone else and buried the body out there and is afraid you'll find it before he can get back to hide it?"

"He could have easily moved a body," Slade replied. "I think someone within his organization double-crossed him, based on the recent body count. He didn't bother hiding those deaths. The Boss is involved in most of the murders we've had in the past few months. Maybe the double-crosser hid something important to him out there."

Her eyes lit with interest. "Keep going," she urged.

"He took Rio so he could find whatever he's after, but he hasn't been able to do that all these months. He got a code from Daniel's watch and used that to coordinate the spot in the Lost Woods. But he only found a small amount of cocaine. He had to realize that having a K-9 officer dog without knowing the commands presents a problem. So he's still trying to find something else out there."

"So now he's coming after us. Can he be that crazy, to think he could just grab me and that I'd give Rio the proper commands to search a dig site?"

"He's that desperate," Slade replied. "Or that stupid. He'd demand you give Rio the right commands so the dog can alert to whatever is out there."

"That kind of lunacy does make him both desperate and dangerous," Kaitlin replied, a sliver of fear shooting through her system.

"We have to get back to those woods and find whatever is out there." He cupped her chin, his eyes holding hers. "We can't rush to judgment on this, though. I have to find proof that Dante's involved before I accuse him publicly."

"Is that what you were doing tonight?"

He nodded. "I collected his hair samples to match to Daniel's. It can't help this case, but…it will tell us if Dante is Daniel's father." He glanced around. "Forget I told you that. I've already done something I'm not proud of, but…finding out the truth will ease a lot of minds."

"I understand," Kaitlin said on a quick whisper. But when she thought of Dante, all of her antennas went up. She'd have to help Slade find that proof, and they'd have to do it by the book from here on out.

Slade pulled her close and she breathed a sigh of relief and said a silent prayer for being safe in his arms. "So what do we do next?"

He stood back, his expression as dark and shadowed as the trees dancing in the hot summer wind. "*You* don't do anything. Just be diligent and watchful and keep me posted on anything—and I mean anything—that seems out of the ordinary."

"And what are you going to do?" she asked, her heart stopping at the thought of him putting himself in danger.

"First, I'm going to let a friend have the DNA analyzed. Then, I'm going back out to that spot in the woods to look around one more time before I put in a request to have a team dig at the site again." He ran a hand down her back. "Meanwhile, I'm going to tail Dante to find out his comings and goings. He'll slip up and when he does, I'll be there to take him down."

"This has to end, Slade," she whispered against his shoulder. "For all of us, this has to end."

"It will now. One way or another."

She didn't like the finality of that statement. "Even if you might have to go after a man you thought was your friend?"

His expression went dark. "I don't like it, but I don't have a choice."

Sensing the tightening in his muscles, Kaitlin put a hand to his face, their earlier intimacy making her bold. "Don't shut me out, and, Slade, don't shut down. You've been through a lot in the past couple of years, but your son needs you. Remember that." She kissed him, just a quick touch of her lips to hers. "And…I need you, too."

"I don't deserve you," he said, trying to move away. "We shouldn't be together." He put his hands on her elbows and looked down at her. "But when you kissed me—"

"No, don't go all captain on me now," Kaitlin replied, determined to stand her ground. "People will always disappoint you, or surprise you, or let you down, but that doesn't mean you have to just give up and shut yourself off from feeling anything."

"Kaitlin, I—"

"Please, Slade, let me continue. We both felt something wonderful with that kiss, no matter how it came about. You felt it, too. Or you wouldn't have kissed me again. God can see you through, Slade. God and me. And even though losing someone you love is hard, you can make it back to a good place." She took his face in her hands. "This, this is real. This is something we can both believe in and fight for."

He put one hand over hers and twisted their fingers together. "Are you talking about saving the world, Kaitlin? Or just me?"

She smiled then, her other hand tracing over his jawline. "If I save you, I do save *my* world. I'm in this with you now. Don't forget that."

"I won't." He leaned down and kissed her again.

And all around them, a dry, hot wind hissed and danced, as if to warn them that they were still being stalked by a sinister force that might overtake both of them.

* * *

Slade handed the tiny gold envelope to Melody Zachary late on Monday. He'd held it all day, wishing he could just throw it in the trash. But the curiosity of wanting answers surpassed his need to follow the rules. So he'd called the detective in. "I don't want to know how you decide to handle this, but it's the best I could do."

Melody quickly pocketed the package. "I'm sorry, Slade. But this is for my own benefit—nothing else. I just have to know. I'll get a friend in the state lab to do a comparison. If Daniel and Dante are related, this will show it."

"But you'd need some of Daniel's hair samples, too."

"I have some," Melody replied. "His room was pretty much the way he left it when I moved all their stuff. I found a comb with hair the color of Daniel's embedded in some of the teeth."

"It'll be a long shot, but worth it, I guess," Slade replied. He'd slept worse than usual this weekend. He couldn't get Frears off his mind. "If the comparison hairs were pulled out and still have a bulb, you'll have a chance."

"My friend is good at figuring out the Y chromosome," Melody said. "It has to work."

Slade rubbed his chin. "I hope it'll bring you some peace, at least."

"You look burned out," she remarked. "I hate putting you through this."

"I'll be fine." He sank down in his desk chair. "It's just a lot to take in. And for now, your theory on Dante Frears has to stay between us. If he is our man, we don't want to tip him off." He pointed to the envelope she'd tucked inside her vest. "That's the last time I risk my reputation. From here on out, we do things strictly by the book. If we don't, we might lose the most nefarious criminal this area has ever had."

He didn't tell Melody that Dante had already pushed him to his limit by taunting Kaitlin. And the worst of that, Dante had a point about Slade's workaholic nature, no matter how blatantly he'd tried to make it.

All the more reason for Slade to stick to the facts and stop thinking about how good it felt to have Kaitlin in his arms.

"I won't say anything," Melody promised. "I'll get this to my friend right away. Thanks, Slade."

He waved her away, then sat staring at the wall. Various pictures and award certificates and trophies showed off the K-9 Unit with pride of place. They'd won awards, fought the bad guys and worked hard to do their jobs. But why would one of their most fierce supporters decide to play them? Had Dante been playing them all along?

He got up to stare at the picture of Frears handing him a check for twenty-five thousand dollars. His friend smiled into the camera but when Slade looked closer, he was shocked to see that Dante's cold eyes held an icy stare. Had his friend lost his soul somewhere along the way?

"I should have been more vigilant," he whispered. He should have watched out for Dante more, should have visited and checked on him more than once or twice a month when they'd get together to watch a game and eat a good steak.

Maybe he could have stopped this.

But when Slade thought back over the years, he had to admit he'd always sensed a darkness in Dante. His friend had a need to be first—that had made him a strong soldier. But it had also made him ruthless and heartless.

"And I ignored it."

Slade had chalked it up to their war years, figuring they'd seen enough death and destruction to give any man nightmares. He'd come home determined to continue the good fight.

But Dante? He'd come home determined to have the all-American dream. Had he gone about achieving that dream through criminal activities?

Slade's cell phone chimed, jarring him out of his thoughts. "McNeal."

"Slade, it's Francine. I…my car broke down on the way home. I have Kaitlin and our canines with us."

"Where are you?"

She named a spot near the Lost Woods.

"On the way." Slade dropped his phone in its protective pocket on his utility belt and checked his equipment. After alerting the dispatcher, he headed out.

On a normal day, car trouble would be just that. Car trouble. But these days—it could be something else entirely.

Kaitlin stared down into the guts of Francine's late-model pickup. "I don't see any loose wires and the radiator seems to be intact. It's not running hot. Give it another try."

Francine turned over the key to test the motor.

Nothing.

"Slade's on his way," Francine called out. She reached back to calm the dogs. Warrior and Francine's trainee Bachelor were in the jump seat.

Kaitlin's gaze searched the empty highway. The sun slanted through the thick trees inside the woods, but soon it would disappear behind those trees and a dark blanket would cover this area. She didn't want to be here when that happened.

"We have the dogs," she told Francine. "We'll be okay."

Her nervous friend rubbed her hands down her arms.

"Yep, but that doesn't help being out here where creepy things go on. People go missing in that thicket, you know."

"We'll be okay. Slade will be here any minute now."

Kaitlin prayed they'd be safe. She glanced at the truck's insides again. Everything looked normal. The brakes were working, at least. "What about gas?" she asked, running to the driver's side of the car.

"I just filled the tank two days ago," Francine said. "And I haven't been anywhere much except to church and work today."

Kaitlin turned the key and watched for the gas gauge to move. "It's sitting on empty."

"Impossible," her friend said, getting in on the other side to stare at the unmoving needle.

Kaitlin pointed to the gauge. "Either you used a lot of gas somehow, or someone siphoned off every last drop."

Francine let out a gasp. "You mean, somebody came into my yard and stole the gas right outta my truck?"

"I think so," Kaitlin replied, turning the engine one more time. "And I don't think we're going anywhere until we get some fuel." Her gaze slammed into Francine's. "I don't like this. Especially if someone knew I'd be at your house this weekend."

"Me, either," Francine said, twisting to look up and down the road. "I don't like it one little bit."

"Warrior and Bachelor will watch out for us."

Francine turned to the two alert dogs. "It's okay, boys. We'll be fine." She petted Bachelor's brown head. "You're my good boy, right, Bachelor?"

The German shepherd woofed an answer.

Kaitlin could see the concern Francine was trying to hide. "We can call the attack command if anyone tries anything, Francine. Okay?"

"I'll call Slade back," Francine said, her finger tapping on her phone, her big brown eyes like chocolate orbs.

Kaitlin heard the roar of an approaching vehicle. "Wait, maybe that's him."

They both turned to stare out the back window.

A big black van was headed directly toward them.

TWELVE

Kaitlin grabbed Warrior by the collar. "Francine, keep Bachelor in line. We might need them both."

The other woman moved her gaze from the approaching van to Kaitlin. "Why?"

Kaitlin took another look at the van. "I think that's the same van. The one my attacker was in the other day."

Francine swung around so fast her silver earrings danced against her cheeks. "The kidnapper?"

"I think so," Kaitlin replied, willing herself to stay focused. "Let's just sit here and see what happens. We can send out the dogs if we have to."

"Okay." Francine kept a tight hand on Bachelor's collar and then took a deep breath. "This is why we train canines," she kept saying. "They will protect us."

The van pulled up behind the truck. Kaitlin realized too late that the hood was still up, a sure sign that they couldn't get away.

Expecting a man dressed in all black and wearing a ski mask, Kaitlin waited with baited breath as the driver's side door opened. But a young man with shaggy, dirty-blond hair got out and ambled toward them.

"It's not my attacker," she managed to whisper before the man came up to the open window.

"Good afternoon, ladies," the man said, a grin on his face. "Got car trouble?"

"We do," Kaitlin replied. Behind her, Warrior let out a soft growl. "But we've called for help. Should be here any minute."

The man leaned close to stare into the truck, his brown eyes moving with radar precision over Francine and the dogs.

"Beautiful animals. Are they for sale?"

Thinking that was a strange and telling question, Kaitlin shook her head. "No. We use them as guard dogs. They go everywhere with us."

The guy backed up to stare at her. "Is that a warning, lady?"

"Yes, it is," Francine blurted out. "And our help just pulled behind your van."

Kaitlin glanced in the rearview mirror and sighed with relief. Slade was out of his vehicle and hotfooting it toward the car, one hand on his gun, his cell at his ear. He'd probably dispatched the tag numbers to get information on the van.

"Everything all right here?" he asked, glancing inside the black van as he walked by. He put his phone away, his eyes trained on the man standing by the truck.

The man whirled around, his hands palm out. "Just thought I'd offer my help. But I think these nice ladies have things under control."

Slade stared the man down. Dirty Blond shifted uncomfortably, sweat popping out on his pimply face. "Sir, can I see your license and registration, please?"

The man looked shocked. And scared. "What? What did I do?"

"Nothing that I know of," Slade said, his tone firm and calm. Kaitlin wondered if he'd already gotten a hit regarding the van. "But we recently had a near-kidnapping involving a van that matches yours. Mind if I verify that your vehicle wasn't involved?"

"I don't get why, man. I saw them broke down and just stopped to help. Can't I go now?"

Slade glanced around toward the van. "You have a broken taillight. I'd appreciate it if you could show me your license and registration."

"Whatever!" The skinny fellow pivoted to head back to the van.

Slade glanced in the truck.

"Go," Kaitlin said. "We're okay."

Slade went with the man to the van, but waited outside while the man leaned over to dig through the glove compartment.

Kaitlin watched in the driver's side mirror as Slade spoke into his radio. "He's doing a license check, I think. If that man's in the NCIC database, the captain will know soon."

"What if he finds something in the national database?" Francine asked. "What if that guy is crazy and pulls out a gun?"

"Slade knows what he's doing. He's going through his check list." She watched as he read over the registration papers.

Then he said something to the other man.

Dirty Blond's eyes widened and Kaitlin heard a string of expletives, but before anyone could blink, he pushed past Slade and took off running straight into the woods.

Slade immediately spoke into his radio, probably calling for backup. Then he shouted to Kaitlin. "Give me Warrior."

She did as he asked, commanding the animal to jump out of the truck. Slade took over from there and gave Warrior the attack command. Warrior sniffed the ground, already tracking the suspect.

"Don't move and don't let Bachelor out of your sight," Slade ordered. Then he dashed into the woods after Warrior.

Kaitlin sat staring at the trees. "I can't believe this."

Francine patted Bachelor and acknowledged the dog's alert growls. "It's okay, boy. You might get to go a round or two if anybody else shows up."

Kaitlin glanced in the rearview again. "I sure hope no one is hiding in that van."

Kaitlin thought about searching the vehicle, but Slade had told her to stay put. And yet, what if someone was holed up in there and they were too scared to get out now?

"Let me borrow Bachelor," she told Francine as she exited the truck.

"No, Kait." Francine held tight to her animal. "Slade said not to move. I'm not moving and neither is Bachelor."

Kaitlin couldn't sit still, waiting and wondering. She got out and paced by the side of the road.

When they heard Warrior's barks deep in the woods, Kaitlin turned to stare. "Maybe I should go after Slade."

"Like you said, the man knows his job and backup is on the way," Francine replied. "Honey, just try to relax. I don't want something bad to happen to you."

Kaitlin nodded. "Okay, but only because I don't want to leave you alone."

"I appreciate that." Her friend kept searching the road. "I hear sirens."

By the time a backup K-9 patrol had arrived, Slade came stomping out of the woods, pushing the now-handcuffed runner along in front of him. The guy's shirt was torn and it looked like he had a bleeding bite mark on one of his arms. Warrior followed close by, trotting toward where Kaitlin stood by the truck.

"Good boy," Kaitlin said, reaching inside the truck to find an old chew toy. "Great job, Warrior-man." A tremendous shudder riveted her body, but she tried to give the illusion of calm.

Slade's eyes searched hers. "Y'all okay?"

"We're good." She eyed the young man being hauled to the patrol car. "What's his story?"

"He has an outstanding warrant. Deadbeat dad. Didn't pay child support. I ran a check and the warrant popped up. He split when I confronted him about it."

"Do you believe that?"

"The database has that information but not much else. I'll make sure he's telling the whole truth," Slade replied. "Let me go talk to Jackson and give him the scoop. I'll be right back." He turned around. "I saw some wrapper papers in a cup holder by his seat, so we'll search the van, too. Just in case."

Kaitlin sighed again. "Hey, Slade. The truck's gas tank is completely empty. That's why we broke down."

He came striding back. "Are you sure?"

"Yep," Francine said as she crawled out of the truck. "I filled it up two days ago. No way I could have used that much fuel."

"We think someone deliberately siphoned it out," Kaitlin explained.

"Sit tight for a second." Slade hurried to the patrol car and said a few words to Jackson.

Jackson and his dog, Titan, did a quick search of the van, but after finding a baggie filled with what looked like a small amount of marijuana, Jackson shook his head. Then he headed back to the patrol car.

Slade turned back to Kaitlin. "Jackson's gonna call a

gas station to bring you some fuel, Francine. I'll stay here until they get here."

"Thanks," Francine said. "I think I'll let Bachelor take a run while we wait. He's as hyped up as I am. Warrior can come, too."

Kaitlin lifted her chin. "Thanks, Francine."

That left Kaitlin and Slade standing alone.

"Are you sure you're okay?" he asked, his gaze lingering on her.

"I'm fine. Just another close call. Do you think that man is connected to The Boss?"

"I don't know. We've got him on the outstanding warrant, resisting an officer and a bag of weed. None of that can connect him to The Boss, though." He stared at the black van. "That sure looks a lot like the vehicle, but there aren't any bullet holes in the passenger door. "I ran the plates. It's not stolen and he has insurance and the title." He glanced back at the van. "We can haul it in and go over it again."

"Good idea. I'd feel better knowing for sure."

He took her by the arm. "C'mon. Let's talk."

Kaitlin waved to Francine and made sure she could keep her friend and the dogs in her sights. And while she walked, she prayed this might at least give them a break in this case.

Because she couldn't take much more of this kind of upheaval.

"Everything checks out, but I still don't like it."

Slade's gaze moved over the unit officers he'd called into the conference room this morning.

Jackson Worth spoke up. "The van could have been cleaned and fixed up. Perhaps sold? Do we know how long that kid has owned it?"

"A few months," Slade replied. "That doesn't fit with what happened here last week, though."

Melody raised her hand. "Could the kid—Rudy Hampton—be lying?"

"A good possibility," Slade replied. "He's a jittery mess. I think he was almost relieved to be locked up." He tapped his fingers on the table. "Rudy has hit hard times and he got behind on his child support payments. Says he has a one-year-old."

"Being down and out can lead to all kinds of deals regarding money," Valerie said. "Maybe he's lying because he has to."

"To protect his child?" Slade mused.

Valerie nodded. "If someone offered him a way out from under that warrant or threatened him if he didn't cooperate, then maybe he might have to lie to us."

Slade appreciated Valerie's perspective since she had taken over raising her own orphaned niece, Bethany.

"How long can we hold him?" Parker Adams asked, his pen whirling through his fingers.

"Not long enough," Slade admitted. "If he lawyers up, he'll be out on bail in no time."

"I don't think he has the resources for that," Valerie replied.

The talk went on about trial dates and plea bargains.

Slade got up to scrutinize the picture he'd taken of Rudy's van. "Maybe I'll try one more time. If I can get him to bargain, we might get some information out of him."

"Couldn't hurt," Jackson said.

Later, Slade called Kaitlin to give her an update. "I'm going to question him now. That kid is hiding something besides an outstanding warrant. I'm gonna try to find out what it is."

Kaitlin was in the break room, drinking a soda. "Good

luck with that. Most of the people you've taken in either won't talk or…they didn't live to tell anyone anything."

"Good point," Slade replied. "I'll call you later. Want me to bring by some dinner?"

"Would it be okay if I came to your house and brought Warrior with me? I'd like to see Caleb, but I don't want to put him in danger."

"Okay, but make sure the cruiser follows you to my front door."

"Yes, Captain," she said with a long suffering sigh.

He hung up with a grin in spite of the burning inside his gut. If he could get Rudy Hampton to talk maybe he could finally get a break in this investigation.

And that could lead to all sorts of possibilities.

Such as him finally bringing down The Boss and… him finally having the nerve to pursue Kaitlin Mathers without any regrets.

THIRTEEN

Slade was in an almost good mood.

Rudy Hampton had copped a plea. He still had to pay child support, but resisting an officer and possession of a controlled substance had been dropped. Since he'd had well under twenty grams of marijuana, dropping those two had been the easy part.

Getting Rudy to talk had been the hard part. He was deathly afraid of someone.

"If you so much as breathe in a fume from weed, you will be arrested, and next time, you won't get away so easily," Slade had told him.

Rudy only wanted to get out and get away. He'd be on probation for a few months, and Slade had even offered to help him find a job. But for now, Slade would settle for the information Rudy had given him.

"Somebody wanted to borrow my van," Rudy explained. "My friend offered me a lot of money to rent it out for a couple of days."

"Who was this friend?"

"I can't tell you that."

"Rudy, I can't agree to this plea if you don't give me the goods."

"Okay, okay, man. He went by the name D.J. And…he's really not a friend. Just some guy I met in a bar."

"D.J.? No last name?"

"I didn't ask, man. He told me—after I'd agreed to loan out my van for a couple of grand—that his boss would come looking for me if I told anyone."

"So you kept your mouth shut?"

"That's right, sir. I pocketed the money and rode a bike to work and back for about a week. I began to wonder if I'd ever see my van again. I'd just bought the thing a couple of months ago. Just now got the title and insurance all straightened out."

"Where'd you buy it?"

"One of those factory places. They were replacing all their old black vans with new green ones."

That got Slade's attention. He jotted down some notes. "What was the company?"

"Bug Busters. Over in that town near the border." He named the other town. "They said they'd sold several of the vans to one person."

Slade's pulse lurched. "Interesting."

"Not to me. I wish I'd never agreed to loan out my van to anyone. I needed the money, though."

"And then today they brought it back?"

"Yeah, today. But D.J. offered me an extra five hundred to do a little more work."

"And what was that?"

"Follow that truck I found today."

"You mean the Ford that was broken down on the road out of town—near the Lost Woods?"

"Yep."

"Did you do anything to the old Ford before you followed it?"

"Like what?"

"I don't know. Why don't you tell me?"

"I didn't do a thing. I just found the truck where D.J. said it would be."

"So you didn't happen to siphon any gas out of that truck?"

"Huh?"

Slade could almost understand someone hiring Rudy to do grunt work. The kid didn't have a clue.

"Did it ever occur to you to find out why you were being paid to let someone use your van or to follow that truck?"

"I know not to ask any questions. Like I said…I needed the money, man. I don't want to start selling drugs, so I thought this might work out okay. I figured D.J.'s boss wanted a big van to transport something and maybe he wanted me to follow the truck 'cause he was tracking a girlfriend or something."

"And you didn't have a problem just following orders?"

Rudy shook his head. "I thought what would it matter, you know? When I saw that same truck broken down, I figured I'd see who they'd wanted me to follow. Thought I might know the person, but I didn't know those two women. Besides, they had big dogs with 'em." He pointed to his bandaged arm. "I hope I don't get an infection from that bite."

"You'll be fine," Slade replied, wondering if Rudy had failed to figure out he'd been bitten by a K-9 officer dog.

"Did you wonder about the people who hired you?"

"No, I saw dollars and I took 'em. I thought maybe I could do whatever else they wanted, but…not now. Not anymore. I'm trying to go clean, so I can take care of my kid. I don't like this."

"And you have no knowledge of an alleged kidnapping last week?"

"No. Not with my van. If they did that, I wasn't a part of it. Am I in trouble for that, too?"

"Not if you're telling the truth." Rudy's body language shouted *scared and clueless*. "And when you got your van back today, notice anything different?"

"It was clean as a whistle. I think they even painted it and fixed some of the dents."

"You're sure about that?"

"Yeah, man. What's going on around here, anyway?"

"Nothing you need to worry about."

Rudy said he wanted to leave. Slade told him he had to stay in the state of Texas for a while since he'd be on probation. Rudy asked for protection. Slade agreed to put a cruiser on him for a few days.

Slade had gone over Rudy's statements in every which way, trying to shake the kid up and catch him lying. But he believed Rudy was telling the truth, as weird as that seemed.

And that meant that Rudy's old van had been the very van used to try and kidnap Kaitlin. Slade had put in a request to have the crime scene team go over the van with a fine-tooth comb to find anything—a stray hair, skin partials, a new scent. Or maybe, a new passenger-side door.

He also reported that someone had bought a whole fleet of used vans from Bug Busters. Was Dante hiding this fleet somewhere? Slade couldn't wait to find out.

He hadn't been able to put a tail on Dante today, but come tomorrow, he'd start watching and waiting. He'd have to be careful, do some of the surveillance on his own time, but the fire in his belly told him he was headed in the right direction. He had a prime suspect. And he was beginning to gather evidence. But it boggled his mind why the bad guys went to all the trouble of borrowing someone's vehicle to do a crime, only to send it back to that person all spick and span. Did The Boss think they'd pin the kidnapping on poor, misguided Rudy Hampton?

A foolish mistake. Now Slade could follow their M.O. He'd have to go back over the other attempted kidnappings and check on those vehicles, too. Stealing and ditching cars, buying old used vans to do dirty work and paying some poor sap to help. No wonder The Boss was so hard to track.

Now there was hope, he thought. Hope for a resolution.

Looking at the clock, Slade decided he'd relax a little tonight and spend some time with his son and Kaitlin.

And come tomorrow, he'd start watching his friend Dante Frears like a hawk.

"That was so good."

Kaitlin smiled over at Slade while they cleaned the kitchen. They'd enjoyed a delicious dinner of mixed beef and chicken fajitas from her favorite Mexican take-out, Roco Taco. Papa had already gone to his room, his night nurse, Jasper, helping him down the hallway. Caleb was coloring pictures in his room, Warrior right by his side.

She loved this. Loved being part of a family. It had been so long since she'd had anyone other than friends and church members to shower with love.

Love?

Yes, love. In the way a friend loved a friend. In the way a mother would love a child. In the way a granddaughter enjoyed chatting with a grandfather.

I can't get attached to Slade's family, she told herself.

It was enough that she was becoming way too attached to the man. She needed to give that some time before she settled into a nice, comfortable routine with his family, in his home.

He's protecting you, she reminded herself.

Things could change once this investigation was over. Her life would go back to the normal, routine workdays and the full but bland weekends. Up until now, that had been enough. She'd never thought past work and friends because she was so afraid to even harbor hope of finding someone to share her life with. Until now.

"What are you thinking about so hard?" Slade asked, one hand on the counter, his gaze fixed on her.

Kaitlin blinked, realized she'd been standing there drying the same dish for five minutes. Should she tell him the truth?

"I don't know. I…I really had a nice time tonight. I almost forgot why I'm really here."

"Because you're a target?"

"Yes. Hard to get that out of my mind, but those fajitas and your family managed to do just that."

"And me? Did I make you forget for a while?"

Surprised, she grinned. "Captain McNeal, are you flirting with me?"

"Maybe. I'm not sure I know how to flirt, but if it's working—"

"It is," she said on a low breath. "But—"

"I hate that word."

She slanted a gaze up at him. "But we both know that being forced together doesn't exactly seal a relationship."

"No, but kissing seals things a whole lot."

"Kissing is nice, but…I think we need to slow down a bit."

"You're not backing out on me, are you?" He leaned close, his words for her only. "Weren't you the one who told me not to shut down or shut you out?"

"I was the one," she admitted, giving him a direct stare. "And I mean that. I just want you to be sure. You've been dealing with a lot of things lately."

"I'm pretty sure I can handle this," he said. "But you're right about one thing. We need to wait until you're out of danger."

"And that means waiting until you find The Boss."

"I'm getting closer," he replied, a confidence in his tone. "Starting tomorrow, I'll be on Frears like a duck on a june bug."

"Rudy came through?"

"Rudy is a scared, down-on-his-luck man who got caught up with the wrong people, so yes, he came through. We've checked him out and other than missing child support payments, he has a pretty clean record. But he's the perfect candidate to be taken advantage of."

Kaitlin thought about her mother. "My mom was kind of like that. She was a very smart veterinarian and she loved her work. But she was so gullible at times. She thought wounded people were the same as wounded animals. They'd strike out because of the pain." She released a pensive sigh. "But animals can be soothed and treated. Humans, on the other hand, sometimes strike out because of evil, not pain. Or maybe their pain turns to something evil. I don't know."

He turned to lean against the counter so they were face-to-face. "And the drug addict who killed her? Was he in pain or was he evil?"

"He was a little of both, I think." She shut her eyes to the awful memories. "He didn't have anything to lose, so yes, that made him do something he might not have done if he could have been saved. But…the brutality of what he did made him evil in my mind."

"So you can't forgive him?"

"I have asked God to help me forgive him, but I won't forget. That's why I love training canines. I get to be around animals and that makes me feel close to my mother.

But I also get to help put away the bad guys, so that helps me to forgive the criminal who killed her."

Slade touched a hand to her cheek. "You have an amazing perspective."

"Not so amazing. It's the only way I can cope."

"I'll get you out of this, Kaitlin," he said, his lips grazing hers. "I promise."

She believed him. He was the kind of man a woman could depend on. She needed to be the kind of woman he could depend on, as well. She needed to show Slade that he could turn to God to help him heal. And to help him find his way back to giving his son all the love he needed.

Slade tugged her close, deepening the kiss, showing her that he was in this for the long haul. He lifted his head and gazed down at her. "Who would have thought—"

"That we'd be here, kissing each other?"

"Yeah. I mean, I've known you for a while now but—"

"I hate that word."

He grinned at that. "But…I didn't act on any of the feelings you brought out in me. Until now."

"And that's why we need to take it slow and make sure we can work through this. I don't want crime and danger to be the only things holding us together."

He frowned at that remark. "I don't think those two things have anything to do with the way you make me feel."

"How do I make you feel?" she asked, too curious to stop herself.

"Safe," he murmured huskily. Then he kissed her again.

They might have stayed that way for a while, except his cell phone buzzed.

Slade pulled back and walked a couple of steps away. "McNeal."

Kaitlin watched as he listened, saw the deep frustration settling over his face.

"I'll be right there."

He put his phone away, glanced over at her, his eyes now full of shock and…regret. "Rudy Hampton is dead."

Kaitlin gasped. "What happened?"

"A neighbor found him on the back deck of his duplex apartment with a bullet hole in his forehead."

"Oh, Slade. I'm so sorry."

He hauled her into his arms. "I let that kid go. I promised him I'd have someone watch out for him."

"What about the cruiser?"

"I don't know. I don't know." He pulled back and scrubbed a weary hand across his face. "I have to go find out how this happened."

"I'll stay here with Caleb."

"Good. You can't go home alone. We told Melody you'd be home at eleven. I'll call her."

Kaitlin hated the torment in his eyes. "No. Let me stay here for a while. I have my car and Warrior is with us. I'll call her after I get Caleb settled."

He agreed, his tone reluctant. "All right. I have to go. Tell Melody to keep texting you every fifteen minutes or so."

"I'll do that right now."

Slade hurried toward the door. "I'll alert Parker, too. And we'll put a cruiser outside. Parker can check things out around the yard. If you need to, get Jasper to help, too."

"I'll be okay," she reassured him.

"Lock the door behind me and shut the blinds."

She nodded, a chill chasing away the warmth of his touch.

Slade turned at the door and gave her a quick kiss. "Maybe you're right. Maybe we can't plan a future until we bring down the criminal who's trying to destroy my whole department."

Kaitlin watched through the window until his truck pulled away and then dead-bolted the door and checked all the windows.

Another long, sleepless night. But at least she had Warrior and she'd be able to keep an eye on Caleb for a little while.

She thought of Rudy Hampton and said a prayer for the little baby that was now without a father. Why did evil people prey on those who were too weak to run away?

"I know how that feels," she whispered. Then she hurried down the hall to Caleb's room. Hopefully, he'd fall asleep quickly and stay asleep right through this latest ordeal. If he asked, she'd have to find a way to explain to the little boy that his daddy had been called back out to work. And…she'd have to find a way to keep herself calm.

Just in case.

FOURTEEN

Kaitlin held Caleb close while she read to him from his favorite book. "You really love this little cowboy, don't you?" she asked when she was finished.

"He's a toy," Caleb explained. "But he gets to be a real boy, too."

"You're a real boy, aren't you?"

He bobbed his head and the scent of his lollipop bath soap drifted through the air. Warrior lifted his head, ever watchful.

"Can Warrior sleep with me tonight?"

Kaitlin wouldn't have it any other way. "Certainly. He might have to go home with me after you're asleep."

"Where's Chief?"

"He's sleeping in Papa's room tonight. He's tired."

Caleb looked up at her with big, wide eyes full of hope and longing. "I wish we could all live together. That'd be so much fun."

"It would," Kaitlin replied, her throat clogging with that same pain and longing. "But…sometimes people who are friends can't live with us all the time. Do you understand that?"

"Kinda. I don't like it, though." He did a little shoulder

shrug. "Daddy says that's why Mommy can't come back. She has to live in heaven now."

Kaitlin's grip on his shoulder tightened. "Your daddy is telling you the truth. My mother is in heaven, too. I miss her every day but I know I'll see her again one day."

Caleb scrunched his nose. "I hope I see my mommy again."

"You will, I'm sure." Kaitlin stroked the top of his head.

"I don't like not seeing her. I wonder if she'll 'member me."

Swallowing again, Kaitlin nodded. "She will never forget you. How could she? You're a special little boy."

He stared up at her with those big blue eyes, and melted her heart. "I love Daddy, but I don't like not being in heaven with Mommy."

"Me, either." Kaitlin thought about her own mother and wished she could talk to her about…Slade. About life and love and hope and grace. "We have to love the people we have while we have them," she whispered, more to herself than Caleb.

When he grew quiet, she knew it was time to let him go to sleep. Kaitlin gently pulled away and settled Caleb on his pillows. "Nightie-night time, okay?"

"'Kay." His eyes fluttered then opened. "Warrior?"

The big dog jumped up on the bed. Kaitlin pointed to the foot of the twin-size mattress and Warrior obediently plopped down, his eyes on Caleb.

Caleb giggled, then gave Kaitlin a sleepy smile. "He's so silly."

"He is a silly dog," Kaitlin agreed. Then she leaned down to kiss Caleb's dark curls. "Night."

"Night. Love you."

Kaitlin stood there, her heart growing so big she thought

it might burst through her chest. "Love you, too," she managed to squeak out. She patted Warrior on the head. "Stay."

Warrior gave her one last look, then laid his head on his paws, his focus on Caleb.

Caleb would be safe with the dog nearby, but she left his door cracked all the same. Passing quickly when she came to the big suite where Papa slept with Jasper on a nearby cot, she said a prayer for Slade and his family.

"Protect them, Lord. Hold them in Your grace. Help Slade to do his job. Stop the killings. Keep Caleb safe and let Your love pour over him."

And help me to figure out how to deal with the fact that I'm falling in love with Slade McNeal and his little boy.

Slade stood in the city morgue, staring down at the lifeless body of Rudy Hampton. He'd already heard the medical examiner's official report but he could see what had happened. Plain and simple. A single gunshot wound to the head. Close range. Instant death.

"This is my fault," he told Parker. "I should have watched out for him."

"You put a patrol car on him, Slade. We can't help that he went out on his back porch for a smoke and got a bullet in the head. What more could you have done?"

"I don't know. Brought him home with me?"

"Don't you already have a growing list of houseguests?"

Slade nodded tersely. "Yes. Guess I can't open up an inn for people who are in danger, huh?"

"No. You've gone way beyond your duty with Kaitlin. And I understand why. We've all had someone we care about involved in this investigation and endangered by it, too."

Overcome with emotion, Slade turned away from the kid he'd promised to help. "You're right. Maybe instead of trying to protect everyone against The Boss, I should just go out and find the man himself. I can end this thing if I do that."

He whirled and headed for the double doors, Parker on his heels. "What are you up to now?"

"I'm going back out to the Lost Woods and I'm gonna dig in that spot until I find something—anything—that I can use for evidence."

"The police chief won't like that."

"The chief doesn't need to know. I'll dig on my off-time."

"I'll go with you."

Slade shook his head. "No sense in both of us getting in trouble. Besides, I need you to check on things at my place."

"Sir—"

"Parker, I appreciate it but I need some time to think about this. The digging will help me get rid of my need to crack somebody's head."

Parker held up a hand. "I don't want that to be me, so be careful. Call me if you find anything."

Slade nodded and headed out into the night. If it took him working until his last breath, he'd find whoever did this. He'd find The Boss. Or die trying.

After checking in with Kaitlin, he told her to sit tight until he could get back home. But first, he had one stop to make.

"What's going on?"

"I can't talk about it right now. Just keep calm, Kaitlin."

"What are you going to do?" she demanded.

"My job."

He was headed out to the Lost Woods when he spotted Dante's sleek, black sedan turning on a side street on the edge of town. Most days, he'd see Dante riding through town and never think a thing about it.

But today was a different day. It was late at night, a time Frears should have been at home with his family.

Slade pulled back, slowed down and decided to follow Dante.

The car stopped at a big, rundown warehouse. A warehouse that looked vacant. He hid his truck down the block behind another building, then got out and hurried through a small thicket of overgrown saplings and weeds back to the warehouse. Hiding behind a fence, he watched as a garage door on the side of the old building swung open. He thought about going to check things out on foot, but decided that wouldn't be a smart move. And he couldn't call for backup—not yet. If Dante saw him, the investigation would get even more backlogged. So he waited, thinking at least now he had a location to connect to Frears.

But what he saw next made him sick to his stomach. A large, black van emerged from around the corner of the building. Then a man dressed in black from head to toe came out of the garage and hurried into the van.

Ski Mask Man.

The Boss?

Slade's heart thudded as adrenaline rushed like a frayed wire throughout his tired system, bringing him new life.

Dante Frears was the Ski Mask Man. The Boss. A criminal, a liar and a killer. His best friend was the man who'd tried to kidnap Kaitlin, a man who'd planted bombs and intimidated witnesses and...killed several people in the past few months.

His best friend.

Slade thought he might lose his supper right there in the bushes. He also thought about confronting Dante on the spot, losing his temper right along with his appetite. But he took several deep breaths and got it together. Where was Dante going?

Then it hit Slade. Dante might know that Kaitlin was at his house. He turned and headed back to his truck, his mind whirling. Cranking the motor, he waited until he saw the black van moving down the main road out of town, then he called Kaitlin.

"I just got a lead on a black van. Be aware and keep an eye out. I'm calling the patrol officer to warn him. Don't open the door for anyone except Parker. I'll be there in a few minutes. I'll explain when I get there."

"I know the drill," Kaitlin replied. "Slade, be careful. Call for backup."

"I will if it comes to that."

He hung up and waited until the van's taillights were about to disappear around a curve. The van wasn't going toward his house, thankfully. Slade intended to find out where Frears was going, though. He might not have a K-9 partner right now, but he had a fully loaded weapon and a new attitude.

Kaitlin paced from window to window, wondering if she should tell Jasper what was going on. Deciding the less he knew, the safer he and Patrick might be, she kept pacing. This could turn out to be a false alarm. No need to get the whole house up and out of bed.

Kaitlin checked the road and saw the patrol car parked underneath a large oak tree, her pulse echoing in a swift cadence inside her temple. She'd been around police enough to know that something was up and she might be in danger.

How much was she supposed to take? Only a week or so ago, she had a life. A life that she loved even if it was sometimes a solitary life. A lonely life. But a good, solid, secure life.

She wanted that life back now, and so much more.

"I'll check on Warrior and Caleb," she mumbled, turning to head down the hallway.

A door opened and she jumped back. "Jasper, you scared me."

"Sorry, ma'am," the big man said. "I wanted to get something to drink."

"Okay." Should she tell him what was going on? "Jasper, if you hear anything or see anyone outside, will you let me know?"

"Sure. Something up?"

What should she say? "A possible prowler. We're not sure. Just be careful. Watch for any alerts from Chief, too."

"I'll get my drink and hurry back to Mr. McNeal. Let me know if you need me, ma'am."

"Thanks." Kaitlin rushed toward Caleb's room. His door was shut.

Fear tightened her throat with the force of a hand around her neck. She'd left the door open last time she checked on him. All sorts of horrible images flashed through her mind as she pushed at the bedroom door.

When she swung it open, her heart melted in relief.

Caleb lay with Warrior, both of them curled up at the foot of the bed. Warrior lifted his head, his big brown eyes trusting and sleepy.

"Thank you, Lord," she said on a breathless prayer. They were safe. Caleb and Warrior were safe. Maybe Caleb had shut the door so he could sneak to the end of the bed and sleep near Warrior. Since she hadn't heard the canine's distinctive bark, that had to be it.

Warrior jumped off the bed and grunted a greeting.

"Hi, boy. You gave me a scare." She patted his head and hit a hand against her thigh. "Back on the bed. Stay."

After checking the window, Kaitlin backed out of the

room, her pulse back to a normal pace now. When her cell buzzed, she let out a frightful breath. "Hello?"

"Kaitlin, it's Parker. Slade wanted me to do a sweep around the perimeter of his house. Sherlock and I walked the front and backyard and made sure the patrol officer was okay. You're safe for now."

"Thank you," she said, her heart still jittery.

But the closed door she found niggled at her fears. Had Jasper shut the door? Caleb, maybe? Or was someone else inside this house?

Slade slowed his truck on the outskirts of town. The black van had circled the city on every back road, some even Slade had never been down.

So what was Dante up to tonight and who was he, anyway? Family man by day and dark predator by night? Did he wait until late at night to wreak havoc on the city? Where was he going now?

Slade waited and watched as the van turned and pulled into one of the many dirt lanes leading into the Lost Woods. Glancing around, he breathed a sigh of relief that Frears hadn't struck out toward his house, but the next breath was edged with worry and frustration. Did he dare follow Dante into those woods?

His cell buzzed. "McNeal."

"All clear," Parker said. "Sherlock and I have done a thorough sweep of your yard, and Kaitlin's got Warrior watching over Caleb. Everything's locked up tight. Everyone is safe."

"Thanks." Slade ran a hand down his face. "I've tailed Frears to the Lost Woods. I think he's going back in to dig but the van's just idling right now."

He watched the woods while Parker gave him an update on Kaitlin. "She's okay. Just aggravated. She wants to go home and get some sleep."

"Only if Melody can meet her there, but let's hold off on the swap right now."

"Not a problem. What about you? Don't you need to get some shut-eye, too?"

Slade lifted his head as one of the side doors to the van swung open. When a man dressed in black stepped out, Slade sat up straight.

Then the man turned and grabbed a leash, tugging it tight.

A big dark-colored dog jumped out of the van.

"Me, I never sleep." He disconnected and held his breath.

Could that big dog be Rio?

FIFTEEN

"Where is Slade?"

Kaitlin waited with a tight-knuckled grip on the phone for Parker to explain things to her but after a cryptic silence, she decided she'd take matters into her own hands.

"Fine. I'm going to get Warrior and I'll find Slade myself."

Parker's stern voice halted her. "Hey, now, don't do anything rash. Slade knows what he's doing and right now he's on the case."

Kaitlin was done with being rational. "Yes, a case that involves me. He's out there chasing a man who might kill him because of me, Parker."

"He *is* doing this for you, but he's also doing this because he's the police captain and he has a lead. He can't drop that because you're worried about him. You know how this works." He took a long breath, the inhale scraping over the static on the phone. "Try to relax and stay calm. If you go out there now, even with Warrior, you might make things much worse."

Kaitlin's helplessness engulfed her with a heat that rivaled the temperature outside. But Parker was right. If she showed up in the middle of a situation, she could endanger not only Slade, but other innocent people. "What can I do? I'm not good at sitting around."

"I'm sorry, but that's the only thing you *can* do right now," Parker replied. "I'll drive around and see if I can find him. He told me he'd call if he needed backup."

"Thank you," Kaitlin said, relief coloring her words. "I'll feel better as long as I know someone's watching his back."

"Good." Parker went silent for a second then said, "You know, Melody has this thing she does when she's worried about me."

Kaitlin listened and thought about how Melody must go through this a lot, even if she was a detective herself. "I guess you both have to deal with this, too. I'm sorry. What's her tactic for staying calm?"

Parker laughed. "Go to the freezer and look for the ice cream. I bet all the McNeal men love ice cream. And so does Melody. That's her coping mechanism."

"Ice cream?" Kaitlin shook her head and let out a chuckle that released some of the tension. "You're kidding, right?"

"No, ma'am. I'm serious. Find the ice cream and have a big bowl."

Nervous energy propelled Kaitlin to the refrigerator. "Oh, you're right. We've got caramel and chocolate chip. Someone in this house *is* serious about good ice cream."

"I know it's around one in the morning, but eat up," Parker said. "And call Melody to check in. She can have a bowl with you and keep you company over the phone. It'll make you feel better."

"Okay, I will," Kaitlin said, feeling better already. In a few minutes, she was curled up on the couch with her ice cream, her cell to her ear. "Parker's a keeper, Melody."

"Don't I know it! He's as sweet as this ice cream."

"Speaking of that, this caramel pecan will add an inch to my waistline."

Melody paused, probably to dig into her scoop of rocky road. "It's either this or punching something."

Kaitlin took in a big spoonful, her brain freeze causing her to squint. "I might do that next."

They sat talking quietly for the next few minutes. They'd just finished up a nice girl chat and their ice cream when Kaitlin heard Warrior barking and growling. "I have to go, Melody. I'll check back in soon."

"No," Melody said tensely. "Stay on the line with me while you check."

Slade followed the man and dog through the moonlight, the hot night sizzling around him like a fired furnace. Sweat pooled between his shoulder blades, but he kept moving in a low crouch and prayed if that raggedy-looking dog was Rio, that he wouldn't alert to Slade's scent. *Not yet, Rio. Not yet, boy.*

After Ski Mask Man left the van, the vehicle rolled into a thicket of oak saplings, probably to hide and wait for instructions. Who was the driver? Slade wondered now, his breath coming in shallow wisps, his hands slippery with perspiration.

What was Dante searching for in these dark, lonely woods? Certainly not more drugs. Unless he had small amounts hidden all over the woods. That would explain why he'd snatched Rio. Did this have something to do with Daniel? The boy died here in these woods. Had Daniel left something behind that Dante needed to find?

Trying to keep up in the muted gray darkness, Slade didn't dare turn on his flashlight. When he heard a dog woof, he hid behind a tree and stilled himself, willing the dog to ignore whatever scent he'd picked up on the wind.

"Hush" came a sharp command. Slade recognized Dante's voice carrying through the trees.

"What you want me to do, Boss?"

Another man. Someone must have doubled back to meet Dante there.

"Since that imbecile Rudy messed up big time, we've gotta get this dog to do his job." Dante started ranting, profanity spewing out of his mouth like liquid fire. "Stupid animal. I need that woman here. She could make him do what he's trained to do. Rudy had her right there and panicked."

"Want me to make the call for action?"

"Not yet. That's a last resort. Things are too hot right now. Let's just dig."

Slade couldn't believe what he was hearing. Rudy was supposed to kidnap Kaitlin? The kid never confessed to that. And what was the last resort call about? Ski Mask Man—The Boss—had just confirmed what they'd all suspected. He needed Kaitlin to make Rio follow commands.

Rio.

Slade's heart pumped anew when he thought about the condition of his prized partner. Rough-looking didn't begin to describe the animal. Dull, ragged fur, a gaunt belly and eyes that looked defeated. From what Slade had seen in the growing dusk, Rio wasn't being treated humanely. He almost charged through the woods, gun blazing, to rescue Rio.

But he tempered that impulsive anger into a pledge. "I will end this." And he'd get Rio back.

Then he'd be able to tell Kaitlin that he wanted her in his life for a long, long time.

Right now, however, he needed to wait this out and see what he could find. Right now, he decided, might be a good time to start praying again, too.

So he waited and listened and prayed for guidance.

Dante ranted at Rio over and over, sometimes going into a rage while he jerked the leash against the dog's heavy collar. He was trying to walk off the coordinates of the code he'd found on Daniel's watch—R 23, L 34, R 12. Slade had to bite his tongue, tears burning his eyes, while he listened to Dante scolding and cursing at Rio. Did Dante think the dog could count, sniff out whatever Dante had in mind?

Slade held himself in check. He couldn't rush this. If he called for backup now, Dante might kill Rio. If that fiend did one more thing—

"We need to leave, Boss. Somebody's snooping up near the road."

"What?" Dante's growl matched Slade's frustration. "What is it with this town? Every time I come out here, somebody seems to be snooping. I thought we got rid of all the tattlers and moles."

"Sir, we need to hurry. It's a big place. Lots of people hang out around here."

More cursing. Then Dante gave a hard tug to Rio. "Get over here, you stupid mutt. I should just shoot you right now and dump you on Slade McNeal's porch."

Slade stood, ready to pack it all in and get his man. But when he heard Rio's sharp bark, he realized the dog had recognized his scent. The bark had been high and light.

Happy. Rio was happy to find a familiar, comforting scent. The dog needed his help. But Dante obviously thought the bark was toward whoever was up by the road.

"Let's go. At least this mutt is good for alerting us that someone is coming."

Slade watched and listened as the two men scuttled in the opposite direction and hurried to leave the woods. In order to save his partner, Slade had to do this by the book. And that meant he needed to wait for backup and he needed to keep a tail on Dante Frears.

"Hang on, boy," he whispered to the hot, dry wind. "Hold on."

He radioed Parker and gave him an update. When the detective told him he was nearby, Slade suggested he get back to the house.

"They might be on the way there right now, but I'm hoping they got scared and called it a night. If they spot you, they'll know we're onto them."

"On my way back now with Sherlock. Are you okay?"

"I will be."

He waited until he heard the van crank and he prayed Dante wouldn't make good on his word to kill Rio. Or anyone else, for that matter.

After about thirty minutes of quiet, Slade made his way back to his truck and grabbed an old garden shovel out of his toolbox. In order to convince the higher-ups and this town that he wasn't going crazy, Slade knew he had to find proof. And that proof was buried in these woods.

"It's me—Jasper. I was just checking on you."

"You startled me," Kaitlin said, shaking her head after she'd spotted Jasper standing in the hall. "Warrior alerted."

Jasper did a quick scan behind him, then patted Warrior on the head. "Smart boy. He sure watches over us."

Kaitlin got a creepy feeling, standing there with the big-boned night nurse. "Yes, he's trained to do that. Where's old Chief?"

"In with Papa. He's about as old as his master, poor fellow."

"But still viable," Kaitlin replied, a sharp fear radiating up her back. She didn't really know this man, but Slade and Papa both vouched for him. So why did she suddenly feel insecure?

"Is everything okay? How's Papa?" She thought she'd crawl out of her skin if Slade didn't come home soon.

Jasper smiled. "Sleeping like a baby."

Kaitlin started to pass by Jasper. She needed to check on Caleb. "Good. He needs his rest." She forced a smile. "I'm okay, Jasper. I'll check on Caleb, then head back to the living room. Slade should be home soon."

"Of course." The night nurse whirled toward the kitchen. "I need a drink of water."

Kaitlin didn't realize she'd been holding her breath until she let out a sigh. "Excuse me." She waited until Jasper had gone into the kitchen before putting her phone to her ear. "All clear."

Melody's words sounded rushed. "Are you okay?"

"Yes, but I'll be glad when Slade gets here."

"Everything all right? Are you sure?"

Did she dare say anything? Jasper hadn't done anything to her after all. "Uh, I'm not sure but…I think so."

"I'm coming over," Melody replied. "And I'm calling Parker."

After making sure Caleb was still asleep, Kaitlin ordered Warrior back on the bed with the boy.

Then in a loud voice, she said, "So, Slade, you're on your way?"

Melody gasped. "Okay, you're scaring me. Yes."

Kaitlin stayed calm, ever watchful while Jasper made noises in the kitchen. "Yes, it has been a long night. I know you needed some thinking time, Slade, but I'm worried. I guess I keep on waiting, right?"

"Stay on the phone with me," Melody said. "I'll call Parker on the radio."

"Sounds good." Kaitlin hurried down to Caleb's room,

Warrior trotting behind her. When she was out of earshot from Jasper, she whispered, "Night nurse. Suspicious."

And that's when she heard footsteps hitting the front porch.

Slade kept digging. He should call this in, but momentum kept him moving. He'd dug a wide square about two feet deep when the shovel hit on something metal. He tapped around, the moonlight guiding him, until he saw what looked like a rectangular metal box.

Now he'd have to call for backup. Now he had something that might provide proof. He touched the radio on his shoulder and called dispatch for assistance, then explained the situation. He'd just signed off when he heard a rustling in the woods. He wasn't about to let these crooks stumble on his find. Looking around, he started gathering some old limbs and bramble to hide the hole he'd dug, then he hurried and packed down the freshly dug dirt enough to hide the hole until he could get back. Crouching, he turned to go back the way he'd come, but gunfire sounded all around him and then he felt the whizz of a bullet ramming into his right shoulder.

Slade went down with a moan of pain, but recovered to quickly grab his own weapon. Crouching low, blood oozing down his dark sleeve, he managed to hide behind a thicket of tangled bushes and saplings. Glancing down at his shoulder, he gritted his teeth to the pain throbbing in a path down his arm. Best he could tell, the bullet had gone through and through. Just a lot of blood and a searing pain that threatened to knock him out.

Then he heard footsteps hitting the dry leaves and old branches, the snapping of brittle wood crushing against the crackling leaves. Someone was coming for him.

Slade heard shouting. Then barking. His backup or his

enemy? With his right shoulder booming out a ripping pain, he managed to get up on one knee, then do a lightheaded stand against the old tree.

Searching for a place to hide, he saw a gnarled limb dangling from the ancient oak. The broken limb would serve as cover until help arrived. He worked his way over to the thick mass of dead leaves and tangled branches and sank down behind the big limb. Then he memorized his position to the path and the tree, praying he could stay conscious. Taking out his phone, he quickly took a picture, the small flash giving out an eerie light for a couple of seconds.

Then he got on the radio and gave his status and coordinates again. Assured someone would hear, Slade could only wait. He didn't have the strength to rush headlong into an ambush.

"Stay there. Help is on the way." Jackson. Maybe the barking Slade heard from a distance was from K-9 Titan.

Slade sank back against the tree limb, weak but still functioning. He heard barking again nearby and breathed a sigh of relief.

"Over here," he called, thinking the team was coming for him when he heard footfalls slapping against bramble.

But when he glanced up, a flashlight hit his face, blinding him. A dog growled, an ominous, dangerous sound. Slade glanced around for an escape route. The moonlight signaled a pale gray beacon on one of the many footpaths out of the woods. Could he make it? Slade lifted up and crouched again. When another gunshot rang out, he returned fire.

The barking intensified just a few yards away through the trees.

Rio?

And Dante Frears?

Slade stood straight, all fear and doubt gone now. He'd been waiting for this showdown for almost six months.

Then he heard more dogs barking up near the road and someone shouting a command.

His backup had arrived.

The flashlight went out, leaving a creeping darkness against the eerie moonlight shadowing the trees.

"Come back here, you coward," he called, his gun held in a grip of pain. "Show your face!"

Silence, except for running feet and a whimpering dog.

Slade sank to the ground and listened to the sound of footfalls, retreating this time. But this wasn't over. He knew the location of that buried metal box. And he intended to go back right now and find out what was in it.

Kaitlin had to get to Caleb. That thought made her turn and crouch low while Warrior snarled and barked.

Ordering Warrior to come, she sank down and started toward Caleb's room.

"What happened?" Melody said, shouting the words.

Kaitlin kept running, crawling down the hallway, the sound of shouts and gunshots echoing outside the house. "Someone's breaking into the house. I don't know where Jasper is but I'm going to Caleb's room. Warrior's right beside me."

"I'm almost there," Melody reassured her. "So is Parker."

"Slade," Kaitlin replied, now near Caleb's room. "Call Slade."

She burst through Caleb's open door, Warrior's sharp barking bringing her comfort. She called another command and Warrior went to work, guarding the door. He would attack anyone who tried to get near Caleb.

Caleb sat up and rubbed his eyes then called out. "Warrior!"

"It's okay, baby," Kaitlin said, diving for the bed and dragging Caleb and his cover down to the floor. "Hold on to me. You're okay. It's going to be all right."

Caleb clutched her shoulders, his stubby fingers grabbing tight. "I'm scared."

"It's okay."

Caleb shook his head violently. "No. No more bad guys." Then he started crying, his sobs starting in a huff and ending in a silent downpour that wet his chubby cheeks. "Where's my daddy?"

"He'll be here soon. Soon." Kaitlin prayed that God would be with them. "Just hang on to me, okay? Warrior will keep us safe."

Caleb burrowed closer to her robe, his little nose wet, his sobs echoing straight into her heart. Kaitlin held him there beside the bed, keeping his head down with a hand over it. Had Jasper been hit? Or was he a part of this?

Kaitlin gulped in short breaths, thoughts of what her mother must have gone through breaking through the terror inside her mind. She would not let this innocent little boy die.

A door opened and Warrior's barks matched another dog's frantic barking. Kaitlin gave Warrior the signal to guard. The dog waited, growling and snarling. She'd issue the attack signal if anyone tried to come through that door.

Kaitlin held Caleb close, protecting him, as footsteps tapped a slow, steady path toward the little bedroom at the back of the house.

Someone was coming for Caleb and her.

SIXTEEN

"Kaitlin, it's me, Parker."

Kaitlin's pulse shifted down with each echo inside her head. "Coming," she shouted. She ordered Warrior to stay. The prancing, barking dog immediately became silent and still.

Lifting Caleb, she made eye contact with the frightened little boy. "It's okay, Caleb. It's only Officer Adams. The dog you heard is probably Sherlock. You know Sherlock, remember?"

Caleb sniffed and bobbed his head. Kaitlin stood, carrying Caleb in her arms. "Let's open the door. Will that be all right with you?"

He bobbed his head again. "'Kay."

Kaitlin took a deep breath and unlocked the door, glad to see Parker in one piece. "Hi," she said, feeling silly now that it was all over. "I'm sorry. I panicked."

"You have every right to panic," Parker said, eyeing Caleb. "Everything is okay." He gave her a warning look.

Realizing he didn't want to upset Caleb, she nodded. "Give me a few minutes. I'll be right there."

"Melody is here, too," Parker said. "And Sherlock is standing guard at the front door. All clear."

Kaitlin laid Caleb back down on his bed. "I need to step outside and talk to Detective Adams, okay?"

His big eyes widened in fear. "I want my daddy."

"He'll be here soon," she promised. "But Warrior will be here with you. He'll bark at me if he thinks you're afraid." She pointed to the door. "I'll be right out in the hallway. I'll stand where you can see me."

"'Kay." Caleb glanced around the room. "Can Warrior come close to me?"

"Yes, good idea." She signaled and Warrior hopped up on the bed. "Right here, boy." The canine scooted close to Caleb, his brown eyes centered on the little boy. "Stay."

Caleb immediately placed a hand on Warrior's head. The dog glanced at Kaitlin then laid his head down, nose to nose with Caleb.

"I'll be right outside," Kaitlin reminded him. Once she could see that Caleb was calm, she tiptoed to the hallway.

Parker and Melody stood huddled with Jasper. The night nurse looked as shaken as everyone else. Maybe she'd only imagined he was acting strange earlier. Jasper was as dedicated as they came and she knew that. She had to stop thinking everyone was a suspect.

"What happened?" Kaitlin asked, her nerves still jangled together like twisted vines.

"We almost had an intruder," Jasper replied in his slow, steady tone. But Kaitlin could see the fear in his eyes. "I heard someone outside so I hurried to the front."

Parker glanced from the burly nurse to Kaitlin. "I saw someone running away, but when I called for them to halt, they just kept running. I sent Sherlock to attack but they made it over the fence. He did manage to grab hold and tear some clothing."

Kaitlin noticed the torn black silk Melody had already

bagged in a paper bag. "That looks like the jumpsuit that man who tried to kidnap me was wearing."

"We thought the same thing," Melody replied. "I think they were trying to get at you again." She shot a poker-face stare at the night nurse. "Jasper probably scared them away when he turned on the kitchen light, then ran to the front door."

Kaitlin saw the disbelief in Melody's eyes. Did she believe what Kaitlin had whispered over the phone? That Jasper was somehow involved. Did he run to the door to scare the intruder…or to warn him away? She'd have to explain to Melody later.

"I'm glad I happened to be in the kitchen," Jasper said, his brown eyes on Kaitlin. "I don't want nothing to happen to that little boy. I love that kid."

Kaitlin figured that at least was probably the truth. Maybe she'd been imagining things. Jasper had been with the McNeals for months—since Papa McNeal had been injured when Rio was taken.

"Then I showed up," Parker said, his tone full of restraint. "Another close call."

"Too close," Jasper said, shuffling around on his big feet. "I need to get back in with Papa McNeal."

"Go," Kaitlin said, her gaze moving from Melody back to Jasper. Had she been wrong about the gentle giant?

"Let us know how he's doing," Parker whispered after Jasper hurried up toward Papa McNeal's room.

"Yes, sir."

Melody moved close to Kaitlin. "Do you still suspect him?"

"I don't know. He just startled me and then everything happened after that. Maybe I'm just being paranoid."

"Or intuitive," Melody replied. "I'll run a check on him, but we all know Slade had him thoroughly vetted."

Kaitlin turned to check on Caleb. "He's asleep and Warrior is guarding him. Let's go to the den."

When they'd all settled down, she faced Parker. "Have you heard from Slade?"

The detective leaned forward on his chair. "I talked to him about a half hour ago. He was afraid something was up so I took off to the woods to help him, but he insisted I come here instead. He was supposed to call for backup. The chatter on the radio indicated help was on the way."

Kaitlin prayed Slade had received that help. "He always goes by the book. I hope he did that tonight."

Melody nodded and gave Kaitlin an encouraging smile. "And you did everything right by checking in with me. That's why I got here right behind Parker."

"Thank you both," Kaitlin said, too shaky to say much else.

"Parker, you have to find Slade. Caleb's asking for him."

Before Parker could respond, they heard a vehicle pulling into the driveway. Parker got up, his weapon drawn, and peeped through a blind slat. "It's Slade."

Kaitlin sank back on the couch, her head in her hands. "Thank you, Lord."

Slade heard the front door of his house opening and looked up to find Kaitlin rushing down the steps and into his arms.

He grabbed her, holding tight with his good arm, her sweet warmth engulfing him. "Are you all right? Caleb? Is Caleb all right? And Papa?"

"We're all fine. A little shaken but okay." She stepped back, then gasped when she looked at the blood all over his shirt. "But you're not. What happened?"

"Gunshot. Through and through." He took her hand. "Let's get inside."

She held tight, her arm going around his waist as they hurried in the door. "He's hurt," she hissed to Parker.

Parker nodded. "I heard the dispatch call, but I didn't want to alarm you unless I heard more." He let out a breath, his gaze on Slade. "Glad to see you're still in one piece."

"I'm fine," Slade replied, shaking his head. "The paramedics took a look and wrapped it for me."

"You need a doctor," Kaitlin insisted, her hand touching on the gauze around his arm and shoulder. "You're still bleeding."

He chuckled at that. "I bled all over the woods so this is nothing. They gave me a shot and some pills to stop infection," he said, grimacing as he sank into a chair and handed Kaitlin the bottle from his pocket. "I've had worse."

Melody cast an uncertain look at Parker. Her fiancé shrugged. "The man's stubborn, what can I say? Slade, what happened?"

"You're taking a pill," Kaitlin said. Then she rushed to the kitchen and got him a glass of water.

Slade took the water Kaitlin handed him, figuring it would save time by not arguing. "I'm going to check on my son and then I'll come back and explain."

Kaitlin's gaze held his, but she moved out of the way.

Slade headed to Caleb's room, a great relief washing over him when he saw Warrior curled up with his little boy. Then he peeked in on Papa. Chief was ever present at the foot of the bed. Jasper lifted his head up. "It's been a bad night, Captain McNeal. But we're all safe and accounted for in here. Papa never heard a thing. He's sleeping pretty soundly tonight."

"Thank you, Jasper. Try to rest."

Slade came back into the den and sank down on the nearest chair. "Long night. I saw Frears cruising through town, so I followed him. Went to an abandoned warehouse on the west side of town, near some old factories. Black van pulled up, probably from around back, after Frears's car went into a garage in the warehouse. Guess who emerged and got in the van?"

"Frears?" Parker asked.

"Ski Mask Man, aka Dante Frears. I should have called for backup right then but I didn't want to tip 'em off. So I followed them to the Lost Woods. They had Rio." He stopped, gritted his teeth. "They were back at the dig site, trying to get Rio to alert to something."

"Did you go after them?" Kaitlin asked, clearly frightened for him.

"Got close, so close I'm pretty sure Rio caught my scent. Didn't have time to do much else after that. Frears got a call that someone was snooping up at the road."

"That could have been me," Parker said. "Sherlock and I were coming to find you."

"But I told you to come here instead." He looked around, the tension in the room palpable. "What happened here, anyway?"

"Long story there, too," Parker retorted, his tone grim. "I got here in time to scare away another prowler. Jasper was in the kitchen and I think the prowler saw him and almost ran right into me when Jasper went to the door. Sent Sherlock after him and ordered him to halt, but he jumped the fence before Sherlock could get in a good bite. I fired a couple shots, but missed."

Kaitlin glanced from Slade to Parker. Slade thought he saw a warning in her eyes, but he was probably too tired to function. "Is there something else I need to know?"

Kaitlin shook her head. "No. I'm still kind of shaken." Another round of cryptic glances. She glanced over her shoulder, then whispered, "Jasper scared me when I found him in the hallway, but I'm glad he was in the kitchen when the intruder showed up. I overreacted toward him earlier. Just nerves."

Melody went to a table and picked up a bag. "Sherlock chased them over the fence, but nabbed a scrap of clothing." She handed Slade the paper bag with an evidence tag already on it. "Look familiar?"

Slade looked up, his gaze latching onto Kaitlin's. "Yeah. Black silk." Was this what she was so wired about?

"So if the intruder was here, wearing the black jumpsuit, how could Ski Mask Man be Dante Frears?"

Slade glared at Parker. "I saw someone come out of that warehouse wearing all black, mask and everything. Just as Kaitlin described it, exactly what I saw the day he tried to kidnap her."

Parker tapped the arm of his chair. "Can you be sure it was him? Or a decoy of some sort?"

Slade knew the answer to that. "I can't be sure, no. But I never saw Dante come back out. Could he have stayed behind, waiting for a report? Yeah, I guess so."

But he'd heard Dante's voice out in those woods. He was almost certain of that. Had Frears spotted him, too?

Kaitlin got up to pace by the empty fireplace. "Maybe they all wear black ski masks and jumpsuits when they go out at night to wreak havoc."

Slade held a hand to his aching head. "I heard him talking. I know his voice. He had time to leave the woods, but he could have sent someone after me. I heard someone traipsing through the woods with Rio. I know it was Rio by the way he snarled and whimpered." He hesitated. "I thought I had Frears on me. Someone shone a bright light in my face, but then we heard shouts and canines barking. They ran away."

"And you thought that was Frears?" Melody asked.

"I was sure it was him, coming to—" He stopped, lifted his gaze back to Kaitlin.

"Coming to kill you," she said, her hand going to her throat.

"I'll never know. They got away." He let out a tired breath. "But I did find one thing tonight. I dug all around where we found that cocaine and I hit on something metal."

"What was in it?" Parker asked.

"I don't know. I heard somebody coming, so I covered it up and tried to get out of sight. Then somebody started shooting and I got hit." He touched his injured arm. Almost got me good. I backtracked through the woods until reinforcements arrived."

Melody jotted her own notes. "Did you go back to the dig site?"

Slade let out another breath. "Took a whole team back to verify what I'd found. It's a small metal box—locked—and it's now safe with the crime scene team. We should know what they found first thing in the morning."

Kaitlin whirled to stare down at him. "Well, maybe they'll leave us alone now, at least."

Slade hated to disappoint her. "Frears won't ever leave me alone. This has become too personal for both of us. We have what they've been looking for now, but I don't know what that is yet." He gritted his teeth. "I have to confront him before he kills Rio and probably anyone who's crossed his path, including you."

"So you'll keep going after him, in spite of what almost happened tonight?" She pointed to his arm. "You got shot, Slade. Your son was crying for his daddy and I couldn't tell him where you were or what you were doing. I was so terrified, I almost let Warrior loose on Parker. Maybe you should let Dante Frears go. Let him take whatever he wanted so badly, and ask someone else to take over this case."

Slade saw the hurt in her eyes, saw the fear and the pain, but he wouldn't lie to her or paint her a pretty picture. "I'm sorry, but I can't do that. The man is a criminal. A sick, sadistic criminal who's supposed to be my friend. He made this personal, but I'll make him pay. I have to bring him in. It's my job, Kaitlin."

Parker and Melody glanced at each other and both hurriedly stood. "We'll…uh…go make some coffee and sandwiches," Melody said as she scooted past them.

Kaitlin barely acknowledged their friends. She stared down at him, her hazel eyes bright with despair. "I know this is your job and…you're so close to bringing Frears in. But that's scaring me as badly as knowing the man's after me." She shrugged, folded her arms like a shield. "He's already tried to mess with my head. He told me you always put work first, but I understand that's your duty. It doesn't mean I have to like it."

Her words, spoken with such conviction, slapped him with a sharp hiss of reality, left him heartbroken.

His dead wife had said pretty much the same thing, but in a much harsher way.

And Dante, his so-called best friend, had warned Kaitlin about the same thing. "I think he's messing with both of us. If he spotted me tonight, then things have just gone up a notch."

Kaitlin folded her arms and blinked back tears. "I don't know how much more I can take." When she looked up at him, her heart was in her hand. "I can't lose you, too, Slade. Not when—"

"Not when we've just begun to know each other," he finished. "What am I supposed to do?" he ground out, hoping she'd think about what she'd just said. He was falling for Kaitlin but he'd always believed she understood how things were, regarding his job. Maybe she didn't, after all.

"You're supposed to do your job, of course. Just don't get so carried away with anger and bitterness that you forget what's important. Your son loves you and…other people care about you, too."

Slade tugged her arms apart and held her hands in his. "I'm going to finish this—for my son, and for everyone. Especially for you, so you can feel safe again." And yet, he couldn't plan a future when he didn't know how this would end. "Kaitlin? Please. Listen to me. I care about my family. I care about you, but—"

She bobbed her head, her eyes searching his. "You've gone beyond your duty in protecting me, but I need this to end so *we* can finish what *we've* started. Promise me you'll be careful."

Slade winced at the throbbing pulse in his arm. "I promise."

"I know you care, but don't go after him for revenge. Go after him for justice. Don't become like him, Slade."

Slade pulled her into his arms. "I'm not him."

"No, you've got a lot of reasons to live." She lifted up, gave him a gentle kiss on the lips, then turned and went back down the hallway toward Caleb's room.

SEVENTEEN

Two days later, Slade walked out to the training yard to talk to Kaitlin. He'd been busy with the details of this case and what they'd discovered in the woods, plus surveillance on Dante Frears. He hoped he'd given her enough time to get past her fears and concerns. She'd been staying at Francine's house and only talked to him when he called to check on her. But even those sparse conversations consisted of him asking questions and Kaitlin answering with a yes or no.

He missed her already and he hated this protective wall she'd put between them. Kaitlin wasn't running away from him. She was running from the pain of her past. And the fear of a future with him. Slade couldn't blame her. He didn't have much to offer. He loved his work and after Angie's death, he'd given up on a personal life other than taking care of his son. Still, he wanted to clear the air with Kaitlin. And he needed a favor from her, anyway.

She couldn't run if they were face-to-face.

"Hey," he said as he approached her.

She was wearing her standard dark khaki training uniform, but she still looked cute to Slade. Better than cute. He'd walked out here time after time over the years and chatted with all the handlers, but these days he was much more focused on only one. That sure was a big change in his life. His feelings for Kaitlin colored his every thought, but he couldn't tell her how he felt until he had Dante Frears behind bars.

"Hello." She glanced at his arm where he'd been shot, then went right on with her work. Warrior cleared a hurdle, then went through some wooden slates on an obstacle course. Kaitlin rewarded him with a play toy and some encouraging words after he'd cleared the obstacles in record time.

"He's improving every day," Slade said to break the ice.

The look she gave him was heated—even hotter than the near one-hundred-degree temperature. But even through that scorching heat, he saw a tenderness. "He's had a lot of extracurricular practice."

So she wanted to be all business and no forgiveness. Fine. He'd have to talk personal with her later. Maybe it was better if she stayed away until all of this was over.

"Look, I guess you've heard what we found in that metal box in the woods."

She watched the other dogs but her response was neutral. "I heard. And I also heard you haven't released that information to the public."

"No. That amount of diamonds—worth millions—would bring out all kinds of criminals. Explains why they needed Rio. Nobody knew where exactly they were buried and even after following that number code we found on Daniel's watch, they still didn't find anything. We're keeping a lid on things so we can smoke out Frears."

She frowned at the trees. "Diamonds. No surprise that all the kidnappings and killing happened. No surprise that you're still trying to bring in your best friend. This is a big case."

She wasn't making this easy, but he needed her help.

"Time to try a new tactic. I need Warrior for one more after-school operation, if you don't mind."

That got her attention. Ordering Warrior to stay, she tossed a chew bone at the big dog then pinned Slade with a gaze. "What kind of operation?"

Slade took off his cap and replaced it on his head. "I know you won't like this but…I need to take him to see Dante. I need to see if Warrior can sense if Rio has been in that penthouse and test Warrior for a reaction to Dante."

She rubbed one hand down the other arm as if to ward off the shivers. "You know he will. That's like asking the man to shoot both of you on the spot."

"Dante is too smart to make a move. He can't be sure what I know, and he has no idea we have the diamonds. He might have seen me in those woods the other night, but he can't admit that without revealing that he was there, too."

"Or that he sent someone there so he could come back to your house and kidnap me."

"True. Either way I need to put Warrior to the test, but I'll really be putting Frears to the test. I'm hoping to push him over the edge so he'll get careless with his next move."

Her cautious guard went down. "That's too dangerous."

Glad that she still cared, Slade remained neutral, too. "I'm tired of this standoff. I'm upping the stakes. I'm going after him instead of him terrorizing my team again."

"What are you going to do?"

Another wash of relief. She seemed to be warming up to the idea. "I'm going to take Warrior to Dante's house. If Rio is there or has been there recently, Warrior should alert. And if he recognizes Dante as the man who tried to take you, he should alert to that, too. But Frears won't recognize any of the signs that I can read."

She pushed at her bangs then tossed her ponytail. "And let's say Warrior alerts differently than you've planned.

What if he shows hostility toward Dante? What are you going to do then?"

"I'll tell Dante he saw a squirrel outside or that he smells the cat. Warrior is still a trainee, after all. I can handle that."

She shifted back, then glanced out over the yard toward the spot where she'd been held captive. "Or you could get shot again."

Hearing the little catch of fear in her voice, Slade didn't dare make a move. Not here. But he couldn't help his next words. "Kaitlin, please look at me."

She raised her head, her gaze hitting him with a fierce emotion that mirrored his own. "My mother died because she wanted to help a drug addict, or would have, if the man had been in his right mind. She thought if she tried to reason with him, she could save both herself and him. Instead, he killed her without any qualms." Her lower lip trembled. "If Dante is behind all of this, then he's not in his right mind. He'll do what he has to do to survive. I can't watch you die trying to bring him in. I can't, Slade. It's not fair. We…we need more time."

Not caring who saw them, Slade took the two steps toward her. "I'm not going to die. I promise."

She pushed away when he reached out his hand. "You can't promise that. No one can."

"I'll do my best," he replied, his heart thudding in his chest. Hating the hurt in her words, he said, "For you, Kaitlin. For you and for Caleb, I will do my best to end this. I want so much, for us and for Caleb. You were right. I have a lot to live for."

"Do you, really?" Her expression hardened again. "Do you want that for us *more* than you want to bring in The Boss?"

He couldn't answer her question without being honest, but when he hesitated too long, she took it the wrong way.

"This is why we have to cool things until…after you bring him in."

"You're asking for the impossible," he said hoarsely. "You have no idea what I went through the day that madman tried to take you. No idea what I've been going through each time a new homicide report comes through on this case, each time someone else is threatened or abducted. The man probably killed my wife, too, because he wanted me dead."

Her frown softened, but her words were low and quiet. "My point exactly. I'm not asking you to give up. I only ask that you stay focused and careful."

"I am careful, for the reasons you've named." He held his hands on his hips, then shook his head. "I sat there in those woods the other night and prayed—yes, Kaitlin, prayed—that God would spare you and my son. I want the same things you want, believe me." He touched his hand to her face. "Right now, I have to do my job and as head of this department, I'm commandeering K-9 Officer Trainee Warrior to help me."

Tears sprang to her eyes, but she stood tall. Calling to Warrior, she signaled for the canine to go with Slade. After checking Warrior's protective vest, she said, "Take care of him. Remember, I did train him for exactly this purpose." She gave Warrior an encouraging pat on the head, then glanced back at Slade. "I understand your job, Slade. But no one ever trained me on how to stop my heart from breaking. And I'm a slow learner. I made a mistake—caring too much about you and Caleb when I can't be sure of our future."

Slade wanted to tell her it was no mistake, that he cared more for her than he had for any other woman, including his dead wife. But she marched back out toward the obstacle course while he stood there thinking about all the obstacles they had yet to overcome.

"Slade, come on in, brother."

Slade stood back, taking in the spacious, elegantly arranged penthouse, his mind wondering what secrets were hidden behind this glamorous facade. He knew Dante was alone since he'd had a uniform watching the building all week.

"I hope you don't mind. I promised I'd bring Warrior by and today seemed like a good time."

Dante stepped aside, his smile indulgent, his icy eyes turning crystal. Then he slapped Slade very near where Slade's shirt covered his bandaged wound. "As good a time as ever. Yvette is out shopping—what else? And the nanny took Emily to the park before dinner. We have the house to ourselves."

Invitation or warning? Slade had already commanded Warrior to stay and be quiet so the dog did exactly as he was told, but Slade had felt an immediate tension in the leash when Warrior spotted Dante. Warrior would show him the truth when all else failed. Trained K-9 dogs didn't know how to lie. They only knew to follow orders or pick up on different scents. But the big dog didn't sniff the air too much so that might mean Rio had never been inside the penthouse. If Slade knew Dante, his so-called friend was probably housing Rio somewhere else in a place that no one would connect to him. But even with surveillance at both the old warehouse and the Lost Woods, Slade still hadn't managed to pin anything on Dante yet.

He hoped this visit would at least verify his gut feeling—that his friend was a high-level drug lord. And he hoped Dante would see that the entire department was onto him now. Slade wanted to provoke him into becoming desperate. It was the only way to crack this case.

"Your trainee seems well behaved," Dante said. He stepped back into the room and casually stood behind a chair. "It's a hot day out there. C'mon in and we'll have a nice, cool drink."

Dante had yet to pet the animal, which Slade found odd, but then Dante was such a germaphobe, he might think Warrior was dirty or something. When Dante went around the kitchen counter, Slade saw that as putting another barrier between them, too.

Dante took his time slicing a lime for his drink. He poured Slade a mineral water then made himself a stronger drink. When he looked up, his face was a portrait of restraint and polite interest. "So this is your new superstar?"

"Yes," Slade said, glancing around, "this is Warrior. He's what we call an all-purpose officer. He's been trained to pick up on both air and ground scents. He can detect the scent of drugs, even if they are covered with another scent, and unearth bodies, as well, no matter how long they've been dead. If I give him a piece of material or an item, he can track that scent to the person those things belong to."

Dante remained impassive, studious, fascinated. But he stayed behind the big marble counter, his hands holding to the marble with a heavy, white-knuckled grip. "Impressive. Would you care for another drink? Something stronger, if you're not on the clock, of course."

"No. I don't have much time. Just thought you'd like to see where some of your funding went. Warrior is an excellent officer. He's already proven himself several times."

Dante sipped at his own drink. "In what way?"

Slade gave his friend-turned-nemesis a direct stare. "He's been on protection duty a lot lately. Involving a case that I can't seem to solve."

Dante drained his cocktail and immediately rinsed and dried the glass, his actions so methodical, Slade's stomach muscles clenched. He smiled over at Slade. "You'll figure things out. You always do."

Slade never took his eyes off Dante. "I intend to do exactly that." Then he patted Warrior on the head. "Would you like me to give you a quick demonstration on some of his skills?"

Dante glanced at the kitchen clock. "Sure. Why not? I have some time before Yvette and I go out to dinner." He came around the counter, then leaned down to reach a knuckle out to Warrior. "Show me what you've got, boy."

Warrior did a low growl and went for Dante's hand.

Anger colored Dante's face a pale red. Stepping back to stare at his hand where Warrior had nipped it, he glared at Slade with a white-hot coolness. "Hey, what was that? I thought you said he's a trained officer."

"Warrior, sit." Slade let the leash go slack and faked a puzzled frown. "Sorry about that. I'll give a report to his trainers. He's still got some issues with breaking behavior. We'll keep working on that."

Dante shrugged, then grinned. "Don't we all have issues? Why don't we try again? Let him loose, Slade. Go ahead."

What was this—truth or dare? Slade unleashed Warrior and told him to search, his gaze locked with Dante's. Not sure what would happen since he hadn't let Warrior sniff anything in particular, Slade waited in the hot silence. The big dog took off through the plush house, his paws hitting the marble hall tiles in a spin. After a few tense seconds, Warrior returned and sat at Slade's feet. Apparently, Dante's penthouse was so sparkling clean even Warrior hadn't picked up on anything suspicious. But he had almost bitten Dante even when he had been under an order to stay.

That told Slade everything he needed to know.

"Glad I'm not hiding anything here," Dante said on a chuckle. "Or maybe he's just not quite ready, huh?"

Slade forced out his own low laugh. "Maybe. But he's getting there. I have no doubt that he'll be at the top of his game when I finally apprehend the next criminal."

Dante leaned back against the counter, his eyes as cold as the white marble behind him. "Well, you be sure to let me know when that happens. I'm all for fighting crime in Sagebrush."

"Thanks, guess we'll get out of your way." Slade reached out to shake Dante's hand. "I do appreciate the funding. Sorry about that little nip Warrior tried to give you."

"Not a problem. Maybe it was a love bite." Dante followed them to the door, always staying a few feet behind. "I hope you find what you're looking for, Slade."

Slade turned, his sunglasses in his hand. He put them on, adjusted them. "I intend to do just that, old friend."

After he was out of the building and down in his vehicle, Slade let out a breath of relief and frustration. He'd thought long and hard about letting Warrior smell that torn piece of black silk before they'd gone into the penthouse. But…that might have tipped his hand too much, so he hadn't let the K-9 sniff it. But it didn't take a lot of investigative sense to know that the conversation he'd just had with Dante Frears had held a whole lot of undercurrents.

They'd just upped the ante.

The next morning, Slade was reading over some reports when Melody knocked on his door. "Got a minute?"

"Sure." He closed the folder he'd been staring at, then rubbed his tired eyes. "What's up?"

"I got back the results for the DNA test," she said on a low whisper.

Slade got up and shut the door. "And?"

"They're a match. One of the hair samples you collected from Frears's brush had an intact root bulb. Same with the hair samples I found from Daniel's things. My friend at the state crime lab verified it this morning."

"Dante Frears is Daniel Jones's father." Slade released a sharp breath. "Wow. That sure puts a new wrinkle in this entire case. Jim Wheaton killed that boy and now he's dead. Did he turn on The Boss? Or did The Boss turn on everyone else?"

Melody nodded, then looked down at her hands. "I think they all double-crossed him—his son and his management team. One of them hid those diamonds and he's been scrambling to find them all this time."

Slade rubbed a hand down his face. "That tells me he had a lot of motive and opportunity for killing a lot of people, including your sister. I'm sorry for that."

Melody looked down at her hands. "I don't know why he killed Sierra, but I'm thinking she must have pushed him too far—maybe making demands or threatening to tell his wife. Who knows? I just know I've lost a sister and a nephew and while this verification doesn't change that, it gives me a reason to keep searching for the truth."

"And we'll get that truth," Slade vowed, getting up to come around the desk. "I'm close, Melody. Very close. In fact, I'm going back out to that dig site today with a team, to see if we can draw Frears out. It's a long shot, but he doesn't know we already have the diamonds." He shrugged. "For all he knows, his diamonds might still be in those woods. Whoever was out there the other night, they didn't have time to search. Frears will be back. He won't give up, even if he does think he got to me by shooting me."

"I hope you're right," Melody said, getting up to shake Slade's hand. "I know you went to bat for me on this DNA thing. I won't forget that, Captain. Ever."

Slade accepted her gratitude in silence.

She turned to leave, then pivoted back. "Oh, by the way, I didn't find anything outstanding on the background check we did on Jasper. Kaitlin can be rest assured on that one. He doesn't have any sort of record."

"Kaitlin suspected Jasper?"

Melody came back to stand by his desk. "He startled her the other night. She said he was acting weird, but she told me to let it go. I didn't, of course. Never hurts to be sure. I think she might have overreacted, but better safe than sorry."

Confused, Slade put on a blank front. "Thanks. I'll let her know."

After Melody left, Slade sat back down, shock numbing him. He remembered Kaitlin saying Jasper had scared her, but…Jasper also scared away the intruder. That didn't add up. Now he could reassure her that they'd cleared Jasper.

But right now, back to this latest revelation. He'd hoped beyond hope that maybe Melody's assumptions about Dante were off base. But…DNA didn't lie. Once they arrested Frears, they could do another DNA test to use as evidence, this time by the book. With all the murder charges lined up against him, Frears could be put away for a very long time. Or worse.

As much as it disgusted him, that arrest couldn't come soon enough for Slade.

EIGHTEEN

"Don't you think you're being a little unfair?"

Kaitlin checked for traffic, then pulled out onto the road before glancing over at Francine. "About Slade? No, I'm not being unfair. I can't take things any further until he solves this case."

Francine reached back to pat Warrior's head, then made a face at Kaitlin. "But you told me you understood about a police officer's life, that you could deal. It's hard work and it's a tough life."

"Yes, I did tell you that," Kaitlin replied, glad to be on the way back to Francine's house. After her friend had alerted Slade as to their whereabouts, they'd had a long practice session with Warrior at a busy nearby park with lots of open spaces and people all around, but now she was ready for a shower and a good Saturday night movie, with popcorn and chocolate. Francine had already rented the movie and they planned to order a pizza.

It beat sitting at her house alone.

"So you understand that Slade can't stop this now. He's trying very hard to resolve this. You've never been judgmental before. I think there's more to this."

They'd discussed this most of the afternoon. "I only asked him to be careful and to consider his reasons for doing this. Technically, he's a K-9 officer. His only duty is when the situation calls for him and his partner to take action. This is an investigation. Melody Zachary is already involved in it. Most of the department is involved in it. But Slade has taken things to a whole new level and that scares me."

"A dangerous level," Francine replied. "And that's the part that bothers you, right?"

Kaitlin nodded. "Yes. I'm being selfish. I want Slade to be safe, for Caleb's sake."

"And for you, too." A statement this time, no question asked.

"Okay, yes, for me." Kaitlin slowed down as they neared the Lost Woods, memories hitting her like dry pine needles. Finally, she let out a sigh. "I think I'm in over my head."

"You've fallen for him."

"Yes."

She could admit that now that she'd pushed Slade away. "I tried not to fall in love, but...we were forced together so much because of this thing, because I was almost kidnapped by a lunatic. And the other night, Slade got shot and I was so afraid someone was coming after Caleb I almost let Warrior attack Parker. I've lost focus because I'm so worried."

"That kind of trauma brings out all sorts of emotions," Francine said, her tone gentle now. "Are you sure you're truly in love? Maybe once things settle down—"

"I'll still love him," Kaitlin said. "I can see that now. And that's why I got so upset the other night. I realized I care too much, too fast. He got shot, Franny. I mean, he could have died."

Her friend stared over at her. "It's hard when you love someone, hard to let them go, hard to let go of control. You loved your mama and you couldn't save her. So you had to turn your pain over to God." She blew out a breath. "Don't you think you need to do that with your fears for Slade? Slade is close to busting this thing wide open from what I hear. And he's got the backing of the entire police force. Let him finish what he started and let God take over where you can't deal, okay?"

Kaitlin gripped the steering wheel. "I'm trying. I've prayed and hoped and waited. My life has been in turmoil for weeks now and it's the same as when I lost my mother. But this is Slade, a man I've always admired. I don't even know what it's like to have a normal date with the man."

"Then you have to hope for that day, a normal day where you and Slade can relax and really have some time together." She punched at Kaitlin's arm. "But you can't do that if you're kind of avoiding the man."

"I hate it when you're right," Kaitlin retorted. "I'll call him when we get home and maybe we can work this out."

As they neared Francine's house, Kaitlin's cell rang. Grabbing it with one hand while she slowed down, she said, "Kaitlin."

"Your dog is in the woods."

"Who is this?"

"A concerned citizen. You'll find him tied up on the Southside path, but you'd better hurry before they come back."

The connection went dead. Kaitlin slowed the van and stared straight ahead. The Lost Woods were about a mile up the road.

Francine gave her a questioning glance. "Well?"

"They said I'd find my dog in the woods. On the Southside path." Tossing her phone down, she said, "I'm going to look."

"No." Francine shook her head. "You know the protocol. You need to call someone. We need backup."

"I don't have time. I have to hurry."

A few minutes later, she looked over at the Lost Woods, a shiver moving down her spine. A movement on one of the paths caught her eye.

A dog.

"Rio!" Kaitlin pulled the van off the road in a skidding stop. "Rio, right there on the path. It's him."

Francine squinted and peered out the front windshield. "Are you sure? I mean, it could be a trap."

Kaitlin glanced to one of the trails leading into the woods, her blood pressure shooting up. "I don't know. The person said to hurry because they'd be back soon. But I'm going to look."

"I'm going with you," Francine replied, already opening her door.

Kaitlin scanned the road and woods. "No, stay here with the dogs. If it's him, I'll call out to you."

"I don't like this," Francine said nervously. "Take Warrior with you."

Kaitlin hopped out. "I don't want to scare him away. I'll be okay and I'll be quick." She started walking toward the path. "Rio? Rio, come. I'm here, boy. It's okay. Come on out where I can see you."

He had to try one more time. The woods had gone cold as far as criminals were concerned, but Slade felt a showdown coming.

In the Lost Woods.

Slade knew he was breaking a lot of rules, coming out here to these woods alone. But he was on his own time tonight and he'd waited until his shift was over, so it shouldn't affect anyone else. He'd gotten so close to Dante

Frears and Rio the other night, he could have whistled and brought both of them running. He needed one more chance. Just one more.

No one outside of the department knew Slade and the crime scene team had found that box full of diamonds. Dante would come back here over and over and he'd get more and more desperate with each trip. Slade needed this to end or he'd never win Kaitlin back. His getting shot the other night had given her cold feet, relationship-wise. He couldn't blame her. He'd had surveillance on these woods and the warehouse since the night he'd been shot and no one had shown back up. Too much heat.

Tonight, he'd canceled the surveillance and told his team to stay away. He wanted to flush out Dante Frears. So he'd had a detective in an unmarked car drop him off up the road. He'd told the detective to wait for him by the car, just in case. Then he'd hiked through the woods, alone, with no K-9 backup. He had a hunch Frears would be here soon. He knew Dante better than anyone and patience had never been one of Dante's virtues.

He'd take his chances and try to lure Frears back to the woods.

And if that didn't work, he could very well be out of options. So he waited till dusk and then hiked to the dig spot and stared into the turned earth. If Dante came back here with Rio, the dog would possibly alert to several familiar scents left by officers and the crime scene team. That would fool Frears into thinking he was onto something.

Slade wasn't sure what would happen after that. He'd either confront Frears or try to get evidence, anything, to prove the man was The Boss. He had the piece of black silk logged in as evidence. If they could match that scrap of material to anyone who came out here, they'd have the beginnings of a case.

So Slade waited and watched and prayed. He'd been praying a lot lately. Mostly for patience, but also for his son and for his father. He'd been caught between the two of them and he had to admit he had not been a happy father or a good son. Too late, he saw the bitterness that had driven him since Angie's death.

His son needed love, not bitterness.

"Time to change that, Lord." He nodded to himself. He had Kaitlin to thank for that. She'd shown him how her faith had helped her but…she still had a crippling fear of being hurt again. Now it was Slade's turn to help her.

"Help me to understand her, Lord. Help me to make her see that we can be good for each other."

Slade's stilted prayers ran a silent loop inside his head while he listened to the forest sounds settling into the night. He'd told the detective who'd agreed to wait for him to park underneath an old shed on the back side of the woods. Frears had come in on the other side last time he was here, but Slade had warned a couple of cruisers to be on the lookout, too. Frears was unpredictable and growing more and more desperate. Slade didn't intend to get shot again.

He wondered why it had to come down to this. Why had his life gone one way and Dante's the other? And why hadn't his friend come to him, instead of turning on him?

When he heard a car door slam shut and angry voices carrying through the trees, he knew the time had come for a showdown.

Kaitlin stood near the tree line, on a worn path into the woods. She could see Francine waiting in the van. When she heard a rustling, she called out again. "Rio, come."

She heard a yelp, then watched in amazement as the bramble parted and Rio slowly stumbled his way through the bushes. But when Kaitlin saw the K-9, her heart did a tumble. "Oh, Rio. Poor baby."

The animal's once shimmering coat was now a dull burnished brown, the color of old rust. He was gaunt and hollow-eyed, but when he lifted his nose and sniffed the air, Kaitlin saw the spark of recognition in his eyes. "Rio, it's me, boy. Come."

Rio was heading toward her when she heard footsteps crashing through the pine needles and bramble.

Kaitlin didn't want to leave the dog. "Rio, come."

Rio advanced another few steps but the pounding of footsteps didn't stop.

"C'mon, boy."

Then she saw why the K-9 couldn't make it out of the woods. Someone had tied him up with a very long rope. Whimpering, Rio strained at the rope, but couldn't get any farther.

Kaitlin took another look at the dog, thought about trying to untie him, but then decided she did need backup. She ran across the road and jumped back in the SUV.

"It's Rio, but he's tied up. I heard footsteps. I need to call Slade."

She had her phone in her lap and her finger on call when someone tapped on her window. Shocked, Kaitlin glanced up and saw the face from her nightmares.

A man wearing a black ski mask and a loose, silky black jumpsuit.

Francine screamed and Warrior started barking. Then Kaitlin's door flew open and before she could do anything but drop her phone, the man dragged her out of the vehicle, a glove-clad hand covering her mouth while her attacker kicked the door shut again. She smelled the leather she remembered from the first kidnapping attempt, her stomach roiling with fear and nausea. Had she hit Call before she'd dropped the phone? She couldn't remember.

Francine. What had they done with Francine? What about Warrior?

She could hear him barking and snarling inside the vehicle. Would he obey a hand signal? She could try. It was her only hope. But when she twisted toward the door, another man dressed in black pushed in front of her. Someone else stood at the back of the vehicle.

"Let the dog out when I tell you to," the man holding her shouted to the guy at the back of the van. "And hurry. I need that stupid animal."

Stunned, Kaitlin stopped fighting and relaxed. If she could make eye contact with Warrior and give him the signal to go, maybe he'd run away into the woods.

Ski Mask Man must have read her thoughts. "I'm going to remove my hand from your mouth, sweetheart. Tell the dog to back off, or I'll shoot him and your friend."

Kaitlin bobbed her head, then searched for Francine in the approaching dusk. The man standing by the van had a gun pressed to the glass and aimed at Francine. Kaitlin gave Francine a long stare, hoping the other trainer would follow orders. Francine's look of sheer terror trembled to a calm and she gave Kaitlin a slight nod.

Had she managed to get the call for help in?

"Tell the dog to calm down," the man growled into her ear, his breath hot on her neck. "And don't do anything you'll regret."

She nodded, already regretting a lot of things. When he removed his hand, Kaitlin took in a big gulp of clean air. "Stay," she called to the barking dog. "Stay, Warrior."

Warrior immediately stopped barking but stood at attention, staring out the back window of the SUV, his whole body quivering, his ears up.

"That's good. Nice." If she had any doubts as to who this man was, they all evaporated in the dry heat. She recognized Dante Frears's calm, cultured voice. "Now, I want you to get the dog out of the vehicle, okay? But I don't want him in attack mode, understand?"

She bobbed her head again, glancing at Francine. Her friend sat frozen to her seat but she didn't look as scared now. Maybe Francine would be able to keep her cool and get out of this alive.

He motioned to the man at the back of the vehicle. The other masked man opened the back hatch.

"Now."

"Warrior, come. Stay."

Warrior jumped out and came to sit by Kaitlin's feet, but she knew the dog well enough to recognize his tightly coiled position. Warrior was on go to attack. Just one word from her.

But then they'd kill Francine.

What should she do?

"We're going for a little walk into the woods, sweetheart."

"What about my friend?" she asked.

"I have other plans for her."

"Don't hurt her, please. She's not involved in this."

"But you are, right? Involved, I mean. You're in so thick with McNeal it makes me want to puke."

"Leave him out of this, too. I can help you find what you need in the woods. My dog and I can and then you can just go—"

He leaned in, his mouth close to her ear, his gloved hand stroking her damp hair. "Oh, I wish it were that simple. But it's not. Too bad, though. You're smart and pretty and you almost distracted McNeal enough to let me get on with things. But he's too stubborn to see what's right in front of him."

Hating that she'd practically accused Slade of the same thing, she whispered, "I can distract him again."

"Too late for deals, darlin'. He's waiting in those woods for me, and I intend to give him exactly what he wants."

Kaitlin's heart exploded inside her chest. Warrior was right there with her, but how could she order him to run away when her friend was sitting in the SUV with a gun to her head and Slade was somewhere out in the woods, about to be ambushed?

When Frears pushed her forward, she looked back once toward the SUV and saw the controlled smile on her friend's face as the sun began to set behind the big pines to the west. Kaitlin turned forward, searching for a way to escape. Rio was nowhere to be found now. An eerie wind stalked through the woods, its breeze tearing at the bent and twisted pines and dry-boned oaks, its touch rushing with a cackle through the saplings and sagebrush. She could almost hear the wind whispering a warning. Run, run, run.

If she did try to run, someone might die.

Kaitlin didn't intend to die in these dark woods.

And she didn't intend to get Slade or Francine killed, either, so she prayed that Slade would see them coming and stop this madness before it was too late for them all.

NINETEEN

Too quiet.

After that echo of activity about thirty minutes ago, Slade hadn't heard a thing except some night creature foraging through the underbrush. Had he only imagined car doors slamming and voices carrying through the trees?

No. His gut told him this was it. So he waited, his mind scrutinizing the details of a case that had kept him awake on too many lonely nights. He thought about Kaitlin and how kissing her had made him feel whole again. Then he remembered her angry words to him, words full of an underlying fear for him. But her biggest fear was for herself. She was afraid to love again.

And so was he.

Or, he had been. Now he only wished he could tell her what was in his heart. He loved her. Somehow, Slade had to make her see that, had to find a way to mend her heart and his own heart, too.

One more chance. He just needed one more chance to make things right.

When he heard a definite rustling that sounded like footfalls over the forest, Slade went into action. He lifted out from behind a tree and listened, the echo of the noises vibrating through the deep woods like a stalking animal. Someone was coming, but he couldn't tell who.

In the end, he didn't have to figure things out.

"Hey, McNeal, you out there?"

Dante Frears.

Slade let out a huff of breath. How had Frears found him?

"I know what you're thinking," Dante shouted, the words distorted and dangerous. "You're wondering how I always manage to stay one step ahead of you, right?"

Slade didn't respond. Let Dante come to him.

"I have watchers, McNeal. Watchers everywhere. It's amazing how easy it can be to bribe people and get them to do exactly what you want them to do." A chuckle, then, "If I can't bribe them, I just knock them out or kill 'em. I didn't kill your detective friend parked to the east, but he'll have a nice lump on his head when he wakes up."

Slade swallowed a lump of disgust and dread, but he didn't speak, didn't breathe.

"Come on, now, Slade. We've fought together enough for you to know I can see in the dark. I know you're here."

The footsteps came closer and Slade heard shuffling. The night creatures scurried away, the nocturnal birds lifted out of their roosts, wings flapping a warning. The wind stilled to a hot, silent blanket that suffocated Slade's senses. Sweat drenched his spine, ran down his face, tickled at his neck. But a cold, hard dread chilled his bones.

"For example," Dante called out, "your girlfriend here is willing to do just about anything I ask just to save your sorry hide."

Silence. Slade swallowed again and prayed, an image of Kaitlin in this madman's arms sickening him.

"Don't believe me, Slade? I have Kaitlin right here, a gun to her head. If you come out and play, I'll let you see her before I kill both of you."

Slade lifted up and stood tall, his weapon at his side,

his mind whirling with different ways he could get Kaitlin out of this alive. "What do you want, Dante?"

A harsh cackling laugh filled the still night.

"I want what belongs to me, old friend."

Slade took a deep breath. "Why show your face now? You've managed to avoid this for a long time."

A ragged chuckle grated against the trees. "Frankly, I'm tired of searching. I know you're onto me since you made it a point to bring a search dog into my home, but I also realized I have some leverage now—I've got something you want, so let's just get on with it."

Slade knew what was coming but he bluffed anyway. "Okay, what's the plan?"

A flashlight shone a heavy beam into the night, temporarily blinding Slade. He blinked and searched the dig site. And saw Kaitlin's face shrouded in shadows and light, her eyes centered on him, her expression frozen in a silent scream.

"Kaitlin." He moved toward her, halted, moved again.

"Stay where you are," Dante said, his features shadowed with an eerie yellow light. Another man stood with him, a gun aimed at Kaitlin. "Stay right there and listen, McNeal."

"I'm listening," Slade said, his words shaky, his gaze holding Kaitlin's.

"First, put down the weapon."

Slade lifted the gun high then slowly lowered it to the ground, marking the spot. "Okay. Done."

"Good."

"Next, my friend here is going to throw you a shovel. You have some digging to do, don't you?"

Slade nodded. "If you say so."

Frears chuckled. "Always so agreeable, so consistent." He motioned to another man dressed in dark clothes.

The man brought Slade a shovel. Slade took it, thinking he'd like to bash it over Frears's head.

"Now, before you take that shovel and dig in the same spot you started a few nights ago, I need to let you know I brought you some help."

Dante stepped forward and Slade saw Warrior straining at a leash. The dog was so obedient, Slade hadn't even heard a whimper from him. But then, his trainer was with him and Warrior would do whatever Kaitlin commanded, even if the animal knew something wasn't right. Warrior lifted his head, his nose sniffing the air. He'd recognized Slade.

"I see you finally found a way to get a K-9 to respond to you," Slade replied, his gaze shifting from Kaitlin to Warrior. "What's the deal, Dante? Why have you gone to so much trouble?"

Instead of answering, Dante shoved Kaitlin toward the other man. "Your ace trainer is going to help me find what's mine. You're gonna dig where this dog tells you to dig, got it?"

"Got it." Slade nodded, but it was for Kaitlin's benefit. He'd get them out of this, one way or another.

"I sure hope you've got it," Dante said. "'Cause right about now, one of my guys is waiting in your house for me to say the word. If you try anything, McNeal, he'll get orders to kill everyone inside, understand? So don't send in the cavalry. Otherwise, your papa, your precious son and…that trainer Francine will all die."

Kaitlin gasped and struggled. "You can't do that. Let them go, please. Slade, tell him he can't do that."

"It's okay," he replied, a solid wall of terror slamming down on his nerves so hard he couldn't breathe. "Kaitlin, it'll be okay. Just do as he says."

"Smart man, wise words," Dante said, holding her in

front of him. "Now, sweetheart, I want you to take your animal here and let him sniff this material."

He shoved what looked like a piece of clothing toward Kaitlin, then held it back. "This belonged to my son." He looked up at Slade. "My dead son. My dead son who double-crossed me, right along with my most trusted associates. My dead son, McNeal. You remember Daniel? You shot him during a bad raid. I know you were sniffing around my penthouse the other night, trying to find evidence. Well, now you have it."

"I didn't kill your son, Dante," Slade replied, a calm coming over him. "Jim Wheaton fired the kill shot. I saw the ballistics report. We matched the kill gun to him."

"Yeah, well, he's dead, too, isn't he?"

"Yes," Slade said, trying to stall. "You've destroyed everyone who did you wrong. What's left? What can you possibly gain by killing an innocent woman, by hurting an old man and…my son? By forcing a dedicated trainer to do your dirty work?"

Dante stepped closer, using Kaitlin as his shield. "I want to make you suffer the same way I've suffered." He leaned close to Kaitlin, sniffed at her neck. "You and your sanctimonious attitude, your do-good mentality. You could never get that being the good guy doesn't pay, Slade."

Slade inched closer. "So you'll make me pay for that? For doing what I think is right?"

Dante laughed, yanked Kaitlin back. "I'll make you suffer because I know you love this woman. You might not know how to show that love and you certainly never showed Angie any mercy, but…at least you'll feel the same torment I've felt since Daniel died. I've waited for the perfect moment and it's here, my friend."

Slade didn't know how to reason with such a man. "Dante, I didn't kill Daniel. I tried to save him. One of your own put that bullet in him. Don't you think it's time to let it go and end this vendetta?"

"No," Dante shouted, the sound lifting over the trees. "No. I came here for a reason. I want what's mine. I can't wait any longer. You're getting too nosy, too close. It's now or never, brother."

He shoved the material into Kaitlin's hand. "You take that dog and you make him earn his keep. You and Slade are going to find my diamonds or die trying."

He pushed Kaitlin toward Warrior. The big dog growled and let out a sharp bark. Apparently, Warrior recognized that Dante was dangerous, but like a true hero, he'd followed orders. But once Kaitlin had him away from Dante she could let go of the leash....

Slade prayed Kaitlin would make a run for it. He had to tell her, had to warn her. Somehow.

But first, he had to dig for diamonds that were no longer hidden in the ground.

Kaitlin held the old T-shirt to Warrior's nose, her pride in the dog's behavior giving her strength to survive. The rookie K-9 had gone beyond his duty, staying calm in a very adverse situation. She had to do the same. Somehow, she had to make Warrior attack once he'd alerted. Just long enough to either get away or call for help. Francine obviously hadn't been able to get through on the phone since Slade had been taken by surprise. So that left things up to Kaitlin, Warrior and Slade.

"Here, boy," she said, her hand on Warrior's neck. "Get a good whiff, okay? Do your job."

"He'd better do a good job," Dante warned. "I still have that mutt Rio to deal with, and I don't have any qualms about killing him, either."

"You've got nothing to lose, right?" Slade asked, the shovel in his hand, his gaze catching Kaitlin's.

"No, brother. Not much."

"What about your wife and child?"

Dante stomped forward. "You shut up about my family, McNeal."

"Oh, so it's okay for you to take my family hostage, but I can't talk about yours?"

"I said shut up," Dante shouted. "I mean it. I'll order the kill on your whole family right now."

Slade didn't speak, but he kept giving Kaitlin reassuring glances. Was he trying to warn her or get her to make a move?

"Let the dog go," Dante ordered Kaitlin. "I want this over with and done."

She whispered into Warrior's ear, hoping upon hope that she was making the right decision. When she lifted up, she shot Slade one last glance and prayed this would work. If it didn't, Slade's entire family and her friend Francine could all die.

She stood, her heart pumping, her gaze on Slade, the unspoken things between them disappearing in the flashlight's high beam.

I love you, her mind whispered. *Trust me.*

Slade lifted his chin a notch, his gaze holding hers. She could see the same message reflected in his beautiful eyes.

And for once, they were communicating.

"Attack," she screamed to Warrior. The big dog jumped into the air and sailed toward Dante, his growl feral, his teeth showing.

Slade turned with the shovel and hit the first man who came at him. Then he swooped down and grabbed his gun from the ground and rolled with Kaitlin, firing random shots behind him while they escaped into the darkness, Warrior's ferocious barks and angry growls filling the night.

Kaitlin heard a gunshot, a scream and then she heard hurried footsteps. Someone was running away. Warrior's barks filled the night, followed by foul language and angry shouts. Did Dante have a gun? His man had held a gun on her, but the other one had stayed with Francine.

"Get away from me!"

"Frears," Slade whispered as he pulled Kaitlin along the path. "Warrior's taking care of business."

Kaitlin wanted Warrior with them. "We have to go back. We can't leave him!"

"Hold tight," Slade said. He pulled out his phone and made an urgent dispatch call. A hostage situation at his house. After a quick explanation and a plea for the first responders to proceed with caution, he finished. "Get the SWAT team ready, but go in dark. My son and my daddy are in that house, along with my dad's male nurse and one of my trainers."

Then he turned to Kaitlin. "I have to get to Frears."

"I'll go with you."

Slade lifted her up and held her tight for a second. "No, run, Kaitlin. Run as fast as you can to the east. Follow the path out to where the unmarked car is parked. Go and get out of here."

"What about you? What about Warrior?"

"I'll find Warrior. And don't worry about me. Just go."

"I can't leave you, Slade."

"Yes, you can. Do this for me, please." He kissed her, then cupped her face in his hands. "It's just him and me now, Kaitlin. Just go."

"Slade, please?"

He turned back long enough to kiss her one more time. "Get help and get to my house. Take care of Caleb for me."

He took off before she had time to think about what he was really saying to her. Kaitlin stood there, staring into the moonlight, aggressive barking and angry shouts echoing through her mind.

Then she turned and ran into the darkness, the sound of the barking dog drifting toward her. The path wound through the brush but it was hard to see much in the darkness. Limbs and weeds slapped at her arms and legs, insects and spiderwebs hit her in the face, but she kept on going. She didn't stop running until she'd made it to the edge of the woods.

When she spotted a vehicle parked near an old shed, Kaitlin stopped to catch her breath. And looked up to find Dante Frears standing there, waiting for her.

TWENTY

Frears grabbed Kaitlin, twisting her arm behind her back. "Stupid woman. Did you think you could trick me? Did you really think that dog would stop me?"

Kaitlin's breath caught in her throat. "Where's Slade? What have you done with Warrior?"

Already, she could hear sirens off in the distance. How much time did she have?

Dante started moving, pushing her along in front of him. "I don't care where McNeal is. And your faithful companion is gnawing at someone else's leg right now."

The other man. Frears had somehow managed to run away while Warrior went after the man Slade had struck with the shovel. Dante had probably used that man as a shield. But where was Slade?

Willing herself to stay calm, Kaitlin asked, "Did you kill Warrior?"

He laughed at that. "No. Stupid mutt's standing guard over my equally stupid now-ex-employee. Not a very good K-9 officer if you ask me. I knew this car was still here so I figured one of you would come running."

She closed her eyes, resisted him while he shoved her toward the road. "Did you kill Slade?"

Dante gripped her arm, his fingers digging into her

flesh. "I told you I don't know where he is, but I intend to find out."

"And his family?"

"Don't worry, sweetheart. I can't pull that switch until I have my diamonds. After that...boom."

Did he mean a bomb? Kaitlin glanced around, frantic for some means of escape. If she could get away now, the backup team would be here in minutes. "What are you doing now?"

Dante jerked her close, his eyes a silvery gray in the moonlight. "I'm going to call your boyfriend, sweetheart. But first, we need to get you out of this heat. This kind of weather can kill a person. Lost in the woods at night, without water. Bugs, snakes, all kinds of sinister creatures."

"Stop it," Kaitlin shouted. "Stop it. You wouldn't be that cruel nor would you leave Slade out there. After all, he has something you need, right?"

He stopped, yanked her close again. "So you know where the diamonds are? You willing to barter on McNeal's life?"

Realizing she'd slipped up, Kaitlin shook her head. "I don't know what you're talking about, I'm just quoting you. We never finished digging."

"Those diamonds aren't in these woods," he said on a winded hiss. "Like I'd fall for that."

"Then why did you try to make us dig?"

He pressed his face close, his eerie eyes shining white. "Once I'd forced Slade to tell me where the diamonds were—those were supposed to be your graves."

Kaitlin thought she'd never find her breath again. Had he killed Slade and dumped him in that spot? Had he already blown up Slade's house and murdered everyone in it?

The sound of approaching sirens screamed with a piercing wail through the night. "What are you going to do next?"

Dante pushed her forward toward the waiting black van. "I'm taking you to Slade's house so you can die with the rest of his family." With each push, his words gritted against her nerves. "I'm sick and tired of all of you."

He jerked open the van and shoved her inside. "Tie her up," he ordered the driver. "And hurry. McNeal has called the whole police department. Like that's gonna stop me."

A man got out and came around the van, then grabbed Kaitlin's hands and started tying them together. Struggling, she shifted on the seat, her right foot hitting on something soft and slinky. Kaitlin glanced down, startled to find yet another black jumpsuit tossed on the floor right by the open door. Did Dante have a whole closetful of these disguises? She sent a covert glance toward the man in the front. Dante was still wearing black and he was busy with his phone. Maybe all of his henchmen wore the same uniform.

"Be still," the man handling her said, his tone low and steady. But she could tell he wanted to hurry and get out of these woods before the authorities arrived.

She only wanted to get out alive. Should she stall and hope the police would find them? Or hurry and pray she could get to Caleb before Dante detonated that bomb?

Caleb needed her.

Kaitlin did as the man asked, sitting up straight and putting her hands up and over to the left so he could focus on tying them together. But while he struggled with the heavy ropes, she slowly shifted her right foot toward the wide, open door and gently pushed the black jumpsuit away and out the door. Maybe someone would find it and take the hint. It was her only chance.

"Hurry up!" Dante shouted. Then he twisted to stare into the back of the long van. "Where is the dog?"

Kaitlin glanced behind her and saw an empty cage. "Rio?"

The young man standing by her hung his head, his dark cap covering his face. "He…got away when I was trying to feed him. Wasn't my fault. He got all agitated and tried to bite me."

"Are you kidding me, really?" Dante lifted his hands in the air. "Get in and drive. I'll deal with you later."

The frazzled underling finished his feeble attempts then slammed the big door and ran around the front of the van. He never noticed the black material lying in a pool on the path out of the woods. Or if he had noticed, he was too afraid to stop and pick it up. The man's hands had trembled as much as Kaitlin's insides were trembling now. Rio had escaped!

Thank you, God, for one bright spot of hope.

Slade's head hurt and his mind moved in a long loop of doubt and worry. He'd at least warned the department about his family and Francine, but he had no way of knowing if Kaitlin had made it out of the woods. Sirens approaching gave him renewed energy.

But he couldn't find Dante Frears.

After spotting Warrior standing guard over the man he'd hit with the shovel, Slade handcuffed the hurt, moaning man to a tree and called for more backup and the paramedics. Warrior had left several bite marks in the man's leg, but he'd live.

After praising Warrior, Slade turned to the man. "Where did your boss go?"

"Don't know. Got away."

Now what? Slade would have never sent Kaitlin off on

her own if he'd thought Frears had escaped. Praying Kaitlin had made it to the detective's car, or that she was somewhere hiding, Slade called to Warrior and rushed through the woods, taking whatever trail he could find.

When he heard barking up ahead on the path, his heart thumped erratically. One of the other dogs? And reinforcements?

Slade took off at a run, his gun drawn. Warrior was already ahead of him. When the canine stopped and emitted a low growl, Slade slowed down. But what he saw there on the path shocked him.

"Rio?" he called in a light whisper. "Rio, come."

The big dog, looking scruffy and gaunt, came barreling up to Slade then danced around, facing the way he'd come. Warrior sniffed at Rio, a low growl showing he didn't like this new twist. "Warrior, stay," Slade said. He carefully held out his knuckles to Rio, his throat burning with a raw pain. "Hey, it's me, boy. Remember me?"

Rio nuzzled Slade's hand, his panting tongue indicating he was excited. After petting both dogs, Slade gently introduced Warrior and Rio to each other. When the big dog woofed and jumped up against him, Slade couldn't hold back the tears springing to his eyes. "Good boy. You're safe now, Rio." Warrior sniffed a bit but seemed to understand Rio was a friend.

Rio, however, pranced in a circle, looking back at Slade over and over. "What is it, boy? Do you have something?"

Warrior sniffed the air and looked at Slade. "Lead," he said, following Warrior and Rio along the path until they emerged on the east side of the big woods. Rio rushed onto a graveled path and stopped before a black blob.

Slade hurried to the dog, then stared down at the garment, relief washing over him. He'd imagined Kaitlin lying there, hurt or dead. With a nearby small limb, he lifted the garment up. Warrior ran up and started sniffing right along with Rio, both dogs on alert.

And no wonder. The black jumpsuit had a giant square missing off one of the wide legs. This had to be the same jumpsuit the prowler had been wearing when he'd tried to get into his house the other night. Had Dante changed out of it and dropped it here?

Or had someone else left it here for him to find?

Grabbing the garment, Slade rolled it under one arm and started off toward where he'd left Detective Lee Calloway. His backup should be there by now. If Lee was still alive, he would have radioed in, but Slade hadn't been able to contact him. Which meant Kaitlin might not have gotten away, either.

When he rounded a blanket of tall shrubs and saw the car sitting where they'd tried to hide it, then spotted officers and EMTs swarming around like bees, he knew something wasn't right.

Suddenly his phone buzzed. "McNeal."

"Hello, old friend."

Dante.

Slade swallowed the bile rising in his throat. "What do you want now?"

"I think that should be 'what do you want, bro?' And I think I have what you want."

Slade closed his eyes, prayed. "Dante—"

"No, you listen to me," Dante said, his words pebble hard and deadly. "I have your precious trainer, Ms. Mathers. I found her wandering around in the woods. She's here with me, inside your house. If you don't bring those diamonds to me in one hour, I will kill her and then I'll blow up the whole place—with everyone in it. Do you understand, McNeal?"

"Yes." Slade could only take one breath at a time, flashbacks of his car blowing up centermost in his mind. He couldn't let that happen to the people he loved. But he couldn't send the squad in with guns blazing, either. Relieved that he'd told them to stand down, he spoke one word. "Yes."

"Oh, and call off that SWAT team waiting in the dark. I mean it. If I see what looks like a cop, I'll take care of everything with one push of a button."

Slade held up a hand when Lee hurried toward him, a bandage on his head. Austin Black was right behind him. "Got it. Consider it done."

"Good. Now I have a helicopter waiting, so don't do anything stupid or I'll have to take the woman with me and drop her off somewhere else, if you get my drift."

"I understand. I'll get the diamonds to you."

"See that you do. I've had enough of you and your self-righteous, noble deeds. You just don't know when to quit, do you, Slade?"

"No, I don't," he concurred, steel behind each word. "And I won't quit until you're either behind bars or dead."

"I wouldn't make threats like that, bro. Since I'm the one holding your woman and your family, you'd better do exactly as I say."

"I will," Slade said. And he'd deal with Dante Frears when he got there.

"One hour, McNeal."

The connection ended there. Slade was in a race for his life. He had to save his family and Kaitlin.

Kaitlin sat tied to a chair. She didn't speak or dare look over at Francine. They'd all been warned to stay quiet.

Frears had marched her into the house through the back, a gun to her head. The big van had barely bypassed the commotion of incoming police cars and an ambulance out on Lost Woods Road. Dante had directed the driver to take a backwoods route out of town that looped back around to the east side of the city. After hiding the van near a deserted house and telling the driver to get lost, Dante had grabbed Kaitlin and started out on foot.

"I'm taking you to be with the man you love."

"What have you done to him?"

Dante jerked her back so hard her head rattled against her shoulders. "I haven't done anything yet. But I will. He's going to make a trade—the diamonds for you and that houseful of people he neglects."

"He loves his father and his son," Kaitlin retorted, her gaze taking in the houses up ahead.

"Bingo. Give the trainer lady a prize." Dante tugged her arm tight against her side, causing her to wince. "We're going to wait for him. One big, happy reunion."

When they came up on a narrow alley behind Slade's house, the whole place seemed shut tight. Not a light on, not a sound anywhere. Were they being watched even now? She didn't dare question Dante. Caleb was in that house and if she could get to him, she might have a chance to save him.

"Don't say a word," he commanded softly as he slowly pushed her in front of him. "Slide open the gate, right here. And remember, I'll have a gun pointed at you and I have the cell phone that will detonate the bomb."

"I understand." She bobbed her head and prayed that God would see her through, then slowly opened the back gate behind the small yard. Even if a team was surrounding the house, they couldn't make a move on Dante Frears because they didn't know where the bomb was or who could activate it. And he knew that.

"Looks like McNeal called a retreat. Good. That means he's finally taking me seriously."

So that's how he'd done it. He'd forced Slade to call for a stand-down. Or worse, no reinforcements at all.

"So we can walk right into the house?"

"Yep. Jasper knows what to do."

Jasper. Her instincts the other night had been right. But she'd never mentioned her concerns to Slade. If anything happened to Caleb, it would be her fault.

"You corrupted a night nurse?"

"Wasn't hard. Those folk don't get paid nearly enough if you ask me. I made him an offer and he took it."

Now Kaitlin's stomach muscles clenched as she thought about all the nights Jasper had been right there, sleeping in the house with Slade and Papa and Caleb. He'd even fooled Warrior, always petting the dog, talking to him with a calm voice.

When she thought of Caleb and how scared he must be, she wanted to slug Dante Frears. But she had to focus on protecting Caleb. If she only knew where the boy was. Afraid to ask, she feared the worst. Dante had hidden Caleb away somewhere.

"How's the happy household?" Dante asked Jasper now that he had Kaitlin tied up.

Jasper looked afraid, his eyes downcast. "Papa's sleeping away. I drugged him pretty heavy."

Kaitlin glared up at the man. "Are you crazy? You could kill him."

Dante's laugh was harsh and unforgiving. "Ah, and that would be such a shame." Then he frowned at her. "Shut up."

Jasper shuffled and stepped back. "I didn't give him enough to kill him."

Dante grunted at that. "Well, at least the gang's all here. And so we wait."

"Where's Caleb?" Kaitlin asked. "Jasper, what did you do with Caleb?"

Jasper shuffled again, cleared his throat. "I…I can't find him."

Dante slapped the gun across Jasper's face, drawing blood and knocking the big man back against a wall. "You stupid klutz. You lost the kid?"

Tears came to Jasper's eyes. "I didn't mean to. He got scared when they brought that other woman here. He saw them."

Dante didn't like that answer. He got in Jasper's face. "You were told to take care of that."

"I thought I did. He was supposed to be asleep."

"Did you drug the kid?"

Jasper wiped at his nose. "No, sir. I don't like drugging little children."

Kaitlin couldn't believe the evil surrounding Dante Frears. He'd obviously taken advantage of Jasper's teddy-bear nature and his need for more money. Maybe she could convince Jasper to help her and the others.

"Jasper, you really don't know where Caleb is?" she asked, not caring what Dante did at this point. She had to find Slade's son.

"No, ma'am." Jasper hung his head, his shaggy hair matted around his face. "I'm so sorry," he whispered.

Frears shoved Jasper away. "Get back to the old man. I don't have time to look for the kid right now. Maybe he'll just disappear and Slade can search for him for six months, too."

Kaitlin shouted a silent prayer to heaven. For help, for control and mostly, for justice to be served on this evil man.

And she prayed that Caleb was safe, wherever he was.

TWENTY-ONE

Slade impatiently nodded while the SWAT team commander and the bomb squad team went over the plan. Jackson Worth stood by with Titan since the police dog was trained in sniffing out bombs.

"I got it," Slade said, glancing around the headquarters parking lot. He'd gone through the chain of command to secure the box of diamonds, signed them out of the evidence room and now held them in a small black satchel. "I get in, give him the diamonds and get him out before he blows up all of us."

The SWAT team commander held his cell, getting reports from the team surrounding Slade's house. He listened, then turned to Slade. "He's there. The team's spotted a man and woman entering the back gate to your house. He's armed."

Slade's heart seemed to burst. "Is it Kaitlin? Does he have Kaitlin?"

The other captain nodded. "Affirmative." He gave Slade an apologetic glance. "Gun to her head."

"Let's go," Slade shouted, his anxiety mounting. Dante knew they wouldn't fire on him if he was using Kaitlin as a shield.

The SWAT commander held up a finger. "He sent two

men dressed in black out the back door. Probably lookouts." He told his men to stand down, but to put eyes on the two henchmen.

Parker, Lee, Austin and Valerie all stood to the side, listening. And they'd each brought their K-9 partners. Justice, Lexi, Sherlock and Kip were all sitting at their partners' feet.

Slade had Rio and Warrior in his truck. He'd get veterinarian Connie Mills to check Rio later. Right now, he could only feed the dog and hope for the best. He had to get his family out of that house.

He glanced at his truck where Warrior and Rio were still buddying up to each other. "I'm ready to roll. I want this over with."

"My men will hold back as long as we can," the SWAT commander told him. "Slade, you give the go signal."

"Got it."

Slade got in his truck and started the short trek to his house, prayers stuck inside the lump of dread in his throat.

"It's now or never, boys," he told the two dogs who'd helped him tonight. "I need you both to be on your best behavior, okay?"

Warrior's big tongue hung out, but he looked official in his K-9 officer black Kevlar vest. Rio wasn't wearing a vest, but he'd stay in the truck anyway. Hopefully, Slade wouldn't need either of them. But they both had a stake in this, too.

He pulled up into the driveway and noticed the house was dark except for a lamp silhouetted through the drawn blinds in the den. Taking a deep breath, he got out and called Dante's number.

"I see you came alone," Frears said. "Good man."

"Let's get this over with," Slade replied, his tone curt.

Turning to Warrior and Rio, he ordered them to stay. He'd left the windows open so they could get some air.

"I'll be waiting at the door."

Slade carefully walked up to the porch. The neighborhood shined in an inky, wee-hours darkness, the sounds of the night playing like a soothing symphony through the trees. He heard the screech of an owl, a car's horn somewhere toward downtown, the pitter-pat of an alley cat running away.

Just a nice, normal neighborhood sleeping the night away, but the surroundings felt dark and menacing to Slade.

Dear God, don't let this maniac blow up my home and my family.

The door flew open before Slade could touch it. Dante dragged him inside, then centered Slade near the opening between the kitchen and den, obviously to protect himself from snipers. His gun pressing against Slade's ribs, he said, "Take a good long look, my friend. This will be the last time you ever see these people alive."

Kaitlin and Francine sat tied to dining chairs in the middle of the den.

Slade's gaze slammed into Kaitlin's. She looked defiant and calm, but he could see her knee twitching. Francine's big eyes widened but she didn't flinch.

Slade scanned the room. "Where's my father and son?"

Jasper shuffled out of the kitchen. "Your papa's sleeping, Captain McNeal. He'll wake up just fine in the morning."

Slade let out a breath. Was Jasper involved with Dante? "And…my son? Where's Caleb?"

Kaitlin's eyes held his and her chin lifted. Was she trying to warn him, or let him know something?

Slade turned to Dante. "I said where is my son?"

"We can't find him," Jasper said, his head down. "He took off when…when things got bad."

"Shut up," Dante said, his tone full of malice. "You are a big stupid goon and if you want to get paid, you will shut your mouth."

Jasper looked embarrassed. Slade's stomach roiled with a new fear. What had Jasper done to his father and his son? Slade shifted, the steel of the gun hitting against his Kevlar vest. "I want my son, Dante."

"I'd like to have my son back," Dante shouted, all patience gone now that he had Slade where he wanted him. Rage shook him, sweat dripped down his dirty face. "But Daniel is dead, Slade. Dead."

"I didn't know he was your son until this week," Slade replied, hoping to stall him. "I didn't kill him, Dante."

"Maybe not, but you went out that night to take him down and you did nothing, *nothing* to help him."

"Did you?"

Dante issued several choice words. "I tried. I gave his mother anything she wanted, tried to show them I cared. But they all double-crossed me—Daniel, Sierra, even Arianna and Gunther, and that conniving Jim Wheaton. Hiding my diamonds so they could go off on their own."

"So you just kept on killing anyone who got in your way?"

"I killed them because they betrayed me."

Slade felt sorry for his buddy. "Even Sierra, the mother of your son?"

Dante didn't seem so confident now. "She kept nagging me, man. It was an accident. Didn't mean to smother her, but I had to keep her quiet. I couldn't risk Yvette finding out."

Slade zoomed in on that, hoping to appeal to Frears's

obvious love for his family. "Yvette and Emily, what will become of them?"

Dante shook his head. "I won't leave them. I'll send for them real soon and everything will be okay again."

Slade stared into Dante's cold, dead eyes. "I can get you some help."

"I don't need your kind of help!" Dante jerked Slade close, the gun digging into Slade's side. "That bulletproof vest won't save you and it sure won't save these people." He shrugged. "I doubt any of us can be saved, huh?"

The man had a death wish and nothing to lose.

"How are you planning on pulling this off?" Slade asked, a calm steadying him each time he looked at Kaitlin. "You've confessed to a lot of things in front of several witnesses. The cops are all over the Lost Woods, gathering evidence, comparing notes. We have an evidence sheet on the diamonds. It's over, Dante. Why don't you turn yourself in?"

"I don't need to do that," Dante said on a sneer. "You'll all be dead the minute I shut that door. And I'll finally be free."

"You'll never be free." Slade wanted to shout that Dante would be the one dead. He had to end this and if that meant letting Frears escape—

Slade's gaze held Kaitlin's. Now he understood why she had pulled away. He had to let Dante go in order to be able to get back to his family and her. He had to put them first. In a weird way, Dante had been controlling all of them, but mostly, he'd been in control of Slade's life. Not anymore.

"Give me the diamonds," Dante said, waving the gun in the air. "I know you've got people out there ready to dive in and save the day, but this is not the time to be a hero. So let's get this over with."

That sounded almost like a request instead of a command. Could Slade do this and save everyone, including Dante? Not until he knew Caleb was safe. "I want to see my son first."

Dante shook his head, sweat pouring down his brow. "I don't know where your boy is. Maybe he's hiding or maybe he ran away. That's the truth, Slade."

Jasper grunted, his eyes shifting to the old toy house in the dining room. One of Caleb's favorite hiding places and thankfully, the open handles on each side would give Caleb enough air to survive. If he was still alive.

Was the night nurse trying to tell Slade something? He glanced at Kaitlin. Her eyes went past him to the trunk.

Now Slade's whole agenda shifted. He prayed Caleb would stay in that trunk. *Dear God, keep him safe. Keep him hidden there.*

But it wasn't to be. Slade heard a little voice calling to him. Then the trunk's rickety plastic lid popped open. "I'm here, Daddy. Right here."

Kaitlin's eyes widened and Francine cried out. Slade watched in horror as Dante rushed to the trunk and tugged Caleb out with one hand. "Ha, ha. What have we here? Hiding from Uncle Dante, huh?"

Caleb fought at Dante. "No, I want my daddy. You're a bad guy. Jasper told me to stay put."

"Well, you're right about that, little buddy," Dante said, holding Caleb up against his chest. "Jasper is going to regret that suggestion—hid you after my men left, did he?" He yanked Caleb up with one hand, gripping the boy around his middle.

"Daddy!"

Slade couldn't bear to see his son being manhandled by Dante Frears. He gave Kaitlin one quick glance then turned as fast as he could and shouted, "Dante, want the diamonds?"

Then he opened the box and threw the diamonds into the air. They lifted up with the flair of shimmering crystal fireworks and started falling like broken crystal onto the hardwood floor.

"No," Dante shouted, one hand holding Caleb, the other still clutching the gun. "No, no!" He put the gun to Caleb's head. "You'll pay for that, McNeal."

Slade rushed forward to grab Caleb, but in the same instant a large dog sailed out of the darkness from the hallway and flew up into the air, capturing Dante's gun arm with a growl and a snarl. Chief! And then he saw Papa standing there, holding on to his cane, his expression grim and determined.

Dante screamed and dropped the gun. Caleb wiggled out of Dante's grip, kicking and screaming. Slade heard the dogs barking in the truck so he grabbed Caleb and shoved him toward Kaitlin's chair. Jasper grasped a frying pan while Slade opened the front door and called, "Come. Attack."

Warrior and Rio hurled out of the open truck window and leaped up the steps and into the house, both of them tearing into Dante's arms and legs. Jasper pivoted around the dogs, avoiding bites until he was behind Dante. Then he slammed the frying pan down onto Dante's head.

Dante fell to the floor, the dogs still snarling around him. "Sit. Stay." Slade and Kaitlin both shouted at the same time. All three dogs sat back and stared down at Dante Frears. Rio let out one more growl for good measure.

Jasper put down the frying pan and started crying, then he hurried to untie Francine and Kaitlin.

Slade ran to Kaitlin. "Are you all right?"

She nodded as she swept Caleb into her arms. "We're fine, aren't we?"

Francine hopped up and hugged Jasper. "Better than fine."

Caleb reached for Slade. "Daddy, we got the bad guy. The one who was in my dreams."

That innocent declaration sealed the deal on this investigation. His son must have seen Dante the day he'd kidnapped Rio.

"We sure did. I'm so proud of you," Slade said, tears burning his eyes. He kissed Caleb and then kissed Kaitlin. "Take care of him for me. I'll be back."

Kaitlin touched a hand to his face. "You'd better hurry back."

As dawn lifted pink-faced and new over the horizon, Slade and Kaitlin stood over Caleb's bed, watching him sleep.

"I didn't think that could be done," Slade said, kissing the top of her head, his gaze on his son.

Joy shot through Kaitlin. They were all alive and together and she was thanking God. "What?"

"Three dogs and a boy all piled up in a twin bed."

"They deserve this special reward," she said, turning into his arms. "It's over."

"Yes." He glanced down at her, then tugged her out into the hall. "Before we go to headquarters to give more statements, I have a statement of my own."

Kaitlin stared into his tired, beautiful eyes. "Oh, what's that?"

"I love you."

She smiled, tears gathering in her eyes. Seemed they always had their serious talks in this hallway. "Really now?"

"Really. Now. And forever."

She wiped at her eyes. "I love you, too."

Hugging her tight, he whispered, "I finally got what

you were so afraid of, why you couldn't watch what I'd become."

"It wasn't that—"

"I placed Dante above you and Caleb and Papa and everyone else. I had to take him down and I put you all in danger just to prove I could do it. If something had happened—"

"It didn't, in spite of everything. And I was wrong to pull away from you when you'd been working so hard for so long." She gazed tenderly up at him. "I know how things work with a lawman, but I pushed you away when I should have stayed by your side. I was afraid, Slade."

"You were amazing," he said. "I'll have to remember to stay on your good side."

She grinned at that. "You can now. You did it, Slade. You brought him down and we're all okay."

"*We* did it," he said, his smile etched with fatigue. "But I didn't make it easy."

She kissed him, then leaned back. "You're a police officer. No one said that would ever be easy."

"I'm going to do better now, though. I promise."

She laughed at that. "The only promise I need is that you will always love Caleb, and Papa and me."

"That's easy." He kissed her back. "And Warrior, and Chief and Rio, too."

"You have a lot of love to go around I think."

"That I do."

Together they walked back to the kitchen.

Francine was cooking breakfast. "What can I say? I'm nervous. And Mama is on her way over, too."

"Oh, boy." Slade grinned at that. "We'll have food for days."

A doctor came out of Papa's room. "He's fine," he said. "Jasper didn't drug him nearly as much as he could have.

Probably what saved him. Just watch him for a few days and keep him quiet."

"Oh, boy," Slade said again. "Can we see him?"

"Sure, he's been asking for you."

Kaitlin and Slade went into the big bedroom. She stood back while Slade and his father had a quiet talk. His father was coherent and proud. "I slept right up to the good part."

"Be glad you did. And, Papa, thanks for saving the day."

Papa McNeal shrugged. "Chief did that. He kept scratching at the door, so I knew something was going on." Then he turned serious. "What will happen to Jasper, son?"

Slade glanced at Kaitlin then back to Papa. "He did help more than he hindered. He sent the intruder away the other night, and he didn't give you too much of the sleeping drug. He also hid Caleb in that playhouse and he whacked Frears with a frying pan. I think he'll get a lesser sentence and probation. He's willing to testify so that'll be in his favor, too."

"The thought of Dante bribing and threatening that poor fellow into drugging me and planting a bomb." Papa shook his head. "But then, Dante did a lot we can't believe."

"Yes, he did. At least Jasper thought better of it in the end. And the bomb squad deactivated the bomb easily, thanks to Titan confirming exactly where Dante forced Jasper to place it under the kitchen sink."

Papa glanced over at Kaitlin. "Did my son do right by you, young lady?"

"He did, sir." She smiled and put her arm around Slade's waist.

"I hope Kaitlin will be around a lot, Papa," Slade replied. "But right now, you rest up."

"Do I smell bacon?"

Slade laughed. "We'll bring you breakfast, don't worry."

When they were back in the hallway, Kaitlin turned to Slade. “So you expect me to stick around, huh?”

He grabbed her close. “I expect you to marry me.”

“Is that your way of proposing, Captain?”

“Is that your way of accepting, Ms. Mathers?”

“Yes to both,” Francine shouted from the kitchen. “Enough already. Come and get some food.”

“And that settles that,” Slade said.

Then he kissed Kaitlin and together they walked into the kitchen.

EPILOGUE

A week later

Slade stood in front of the big white board that had "dogged" him for six long months. "We now know that Dante Frears, aka The Boss, had several underlings working for him. He bought a fleet of used black vans and insisted his team all wear black from head to toe. While he mostly wore the black silk jumpsuits and did some prowling himself, he rotated his cohorts so none of us, including our K-9 officers, could catch a scent. We had a few breaks here and there, but he finally got too desperate and he slipped up. He murdered a lot of people in the process. But we'll leave all that up to the evidence and a jury. We can clear this off the board now, boys and girls. This case is closed."

A round of applause filled the conference room. Slade glanced around at the five other human members of their team: Austin Black, Lee Calloway, Valerie Salgado, Jackson Worth and Parker Adams.

"I want to thank each of you for contributing to this investigation," Slade said, his smile real for a change. "I know you all went way beyond what's expected of a K-9 officer and I will always appreciate that. We have some amazing animals working with us and I'm blessed that we have some of the best trainers in the country."

"Especially Kaitlin Mathers, right, boss?" Austin said with a grin.

"Right, Detective Black." Slade laughed and shook his head. "I have to say if there is anything good about this tragic case, well, at least we all found life partners. Can't figure that one out, but I'm sure we can all agree that God had a hand in this."

"Amen" came the shouts amid laughter and teasing.

"I can't keep up with who's married and who's engaged," Slade admitted. "But I promise I'll be there with those of you planning to get married."

"And we'll be there for your wedding, Captain," Valerie said, clapping her hands.

Slade nodded, then turned serious. "My former best friend, Dante Frears, will be paying for his crimes. He fooled a lot of us but we made it through. We became more than just the K-9 Unit of the Sagebrush Police Department. We were patrols, detectives, investigators and all-purpose officers, just like Warrior and Rio and the rest of our partners. I'm proud of this department."

After that, he went over the facts regarding the case, how Dante had used one of his businesses as a front for drug trafficking. The stable of black vans had come from an out-of-town business and so had the black silk jumpsuits. He'd bought the ski masks and fake contacts off the internet and Slade had receipts and records to prove all of it. Frears would go down for everything from drug trafficking to kidnapping to bombings and murders. He could get the final sentence—death.

Slade hated it, but justice was done. He planned to visit Dante in prison, maybe to find answers and maybe to give his friend one last shred of forgiveness. Kaitlin had taught him about forgiveness.

After the meeting ended and everyone had gone their separate ways, Slade started cleaning up the board. When he heard a friendly bark behind him, he turned to find Rio and Warrior standing at the door with Kaitlin.

"Hello," he said, smiling. He still couldn't believe he'd found this woman.

"Hello yourself. How did your meeting go?"

"Good." He motioned for the woman and two dogs to come over. Slade petted the animals then grabbed hold of Kaitlin and held her tight in his arms. "But I like this part better."

She laid her head on his shoulder. "I've been thinking."

"Uh-oh." He kissed her hair. "About what?"

She looked up and into his eyes. "I…I might be interested in returning to the force, as a K-9 officer, if that's not against policy."

Surprised, he drew back. "Are you kidding?"

"No, I'm not. I…thought I'd lost all my fears, but I discovered if you're not scared, just a little bit, you're probably still hiding something. I was afraid to put myself out there on the line with you, but now I think I need to be right there on the front line. Fearful but careful, and very sure."

Slade knew he couldn't talk her out of this and he had to admit, he was proud of her. "So…we'd be a houseful of K-9 officers."

"Yes, three dogs, two active officers, one retired officer and…maybe a future officer. Or two."

"Sounds like fun to me." Slade pulled her close and kissed her. "Wanna go out for dinner?"

She nodded, laughed. "Sure. We can talk about our engagement party."

"Engagement party? I have to buy you a ring first."

"You will. But…about the party. I'd like to have it right here out on the training yard."

He chuckled as they started out the doors, the K-9s right behind them. "Fancy. I like that."

She smiled up at him. "Yes, sir. Very fancy. Doggie treats and hot dogs, cupcakes and ice cream. Chew toys and barbecue. The works."

Slade leaned down to kiss her. "Perfect."

She giggled then touched a hand to his face. "For now, I suggest you go home and finally get some rest. Get a good night's sleep."

Slade tugged her back into his arms. "Don't you know, Trainer Mathers—I never sleep."

Then he kissed her to show her he had something else in mind. He wanted to cuddle with the woman he loved. Starting right now.

Behind them, Warrior woofed and Rio did a little tapping spin and gave them a big, happy doggy smile.

* * * * *

Dear Reader,

I have always loved and admired K-9 dogs. They are so brave and so willing to help their partners. I hope you enjoyed this series about Texas K-9 officers. The men and women who train and work with these animals have a special place in my heart. It was an honor to be a part of these stories.

Slade and Kaitlin both had issues from their past that hindered them in this story. But together, and with a bit of grace from God, they managed to push through the bad memories and mistakes from their past to find each other and a strong faith. Slade's friend Dante suffered because he was bitter and angry, and he resented Slade's calm, honorable demeanor. I hope this is a lesson for anyone who seeks retribution rather than redemption. God's love is always stronger than bitterness and anger.

May the angels watch over you. Always.

Lenora Worth

Questions for Discussion

1. Slade held a certain guilt after his wife's death. How can people cope when they have grief and guilt after losing a loved one?

2. Kaitlin started training K-9 dogs after the death of her mother. Do you think this helped her get over her grief?

3. Dante was bitter and sinister. Do you understand his motives or do you think he truly was evil?

4. Have you ever known someone like Kaitlin, who turned her grief to good and tried to hold on to her faith no matter what? What can we learn from this?

5. Slade and Dante served together to defend their country, but they took different directions in life. Have you ever known someone who suffered after going to war?

6. Kaitlin wanted to get to know Slade better, since she helped counsel his young son, Caleb. Do you think Caleb played a part in bringing them together?

7. Slade struggled with doing the right thing and trying to corner a sinister enemy. Do you think he handled things in a proper way?

8. What do you think about the relationship between Slade and his father? Have you known a father and son who have been at odds? Did they find a common ground?

9. Kaitlin didn't have any immediate family to guide her. Why was it so important that she depend on her coworkers and her church for support?

10. It took a while for Slade to accept that the man he called friend was evil. Have you ever been betrayed by a close friend?

11. Kaitlin decided she'd like to advance to being a K-9 officer. Do you believe she can balance this with being a wife and mother?

12. Do you know someone who is good with animals? What special qualities does that take? Why was Kaitlin's work so important to her?

13. Slade wanted to protect both Kaitlin and his young son. Do you think he handled things in the correct way?

14. How did Slade's faith grow stronger in this story? Do you think he had faith but it had weakened?

15. Kaitlin and Slade would be working together even after they were married. How do you think spouses working together would work out for them?

Love Inspired®
SUSPENSE

The pavement outside the Kansas City airport radiated heat even though the sun had already sunk below the horizon. Tate held his seven-year-old daughter's hand a little tighter and squinted against the dying sunshine to read the signs hanging overhead.

"That's it down there," he said, pointing. "Baggage Claim A."

Lily Farnsworth was the last of six new business owners to arrive, each selected by the Save Our Street Committee of the town of Bygones. As a member of the committee, Tate had been asked to meet her at the airport in Kansas City and transport her to Bygones. With the grand opening just a week away, most of the shop owners had been at work preparing their stores for some time already, but Ms. Farnsworth had delayed until after her sister's wedding, assuring the committee that a florist's shop required less preparation than some retail businesses. Tate hoped she was right.

He still wasn't convinced that this scheme, financed by a mysterious, anonymous donor, would work, but if something didn't revive the financial fortunes of Bygones—and soon—their small town would become just another ghost town on the north central plains.

Isabella stopped before the automatic doors and waited

for him to catch up. They entered the cool building together. A pair of gleaming luggage carousels occupied the open space, both vacant. A few people milled about. Among them was a tall, pretty woman with long blond hair and round tortoiseshell glasses. She was perched atop a veritable mountain of luggage. She wore black ballet slippers and white knit leggings beneath a gossamery blue dress with fluttery sleeves and hems. Her very long hair was parted in the middle and waved about her face and shoulders. He felt the insane urge to look more closely behind the lenses of her glasses, but of course he would not.

He turned away, the better to resist the urge to stare, and scanned the building for anyone who might be his florist.

One by one, the possibilities faded away. Finally Isabella gave him that look that said, "Dad, you're being a goof again." She slipped her little hand into his, and he sighed inwardly. Turning, he walked the few yards to the luggage mountain and swept off his straw cowboy hat.

"Are you Lily Farnsworth?"

To find out if Bygones can turn itself around,
pick up LOVE IN BLOOM
wherever Love Inspired books are sold.

LIEXP7823